Chris Higgins

Telling You Straight

TAPAS & TEARS

Hodder
Children's
Books

A division of Hachette Children's Books

For Ella

Thanks to the girls for the idea
and their dad for listening.

I never wanted to go on exchange in the first place. When Miss Martínez gave out the letters I wasn't going to bother to take one but Fern grabbed two and passed one to me.

'Wow!' she breathes, her eyes lighting up as she scans the information. 'A fortnight in Spain! I can't believe it. And it's dead cheap. Count me and Jaime in, Miss.'

'You'd better ask your parents first,' warns our new languages teacher. 'That's what the parental consent forms are for. You stay with a Spanish student in their own home but then you have to put them up in return. It's a big commitment. That's how we manage to keep the costs down.'

'Wicked! Do we get to choose who we stay with?' asks Fern excitedly. 'Bags me the good-looking guy!'

'Sorry,' says Miss Martínez sternly. 'Girls will be placed with girls and boys with boys. And, by the way, I'll be coming as well to keep an eye on you all.'

A universal groan ripples round the classroom in a Mexican wave of sound but actually, nobody really minds. In fact, Miss Martínez coming on the trip is a plus as far as I'm concerned. She's young and pretty, with long dark hair and a great figure, but she's no push-over. When she'd started, the boys thought they'd try it on but she was having none of it and had soon cut them down to size. She didn't take any stick from the more bitchy girls in the class either. Now she's shown who's boss, she's loosened up a bit, but you still wouldn't mess with her. At least you knew she'd be able to keep everyone on a tight rein.

That's important in our school. We've suffered a lot in the past from teachers who can't control us. It's not that we're that bad, it's just that my class is particularly noisy and there are a few kids who will always try their luck if they think they can get away with it. Like Jason and Adam and Holly. And Fern, to a degree, though she's more loud than bad. Before you know it, they've gone too far and the teacher's lost it and then we all get the blame and the whole class is slammed into detention which is JUST NOT FAIR!

Even the naughty kids recognize this and say things like, 'It was me, Sir, not the rest of the class,' or 'It's not Jaime's fault, she never does anything wrong,' which is true. Not because I'm a goody two shoes by nature, I hasten to add, but because I would rather die than draw attention to myself.

But teachers, especially supplies who we get a lot of as some of the staff in our school make a habit of being off sick, see it as a sign of weakness to back down when students helpfully point out to them that they are being unfair. So we all get banged into detention on a weekly basis which is very annoying indeed, especially when, like me, you haven't done a thing. But I could no more point this out than walk naked into assembly, which is one of my regular nightmares, so I leave it to Mum to complain at parents' evenings.

Anyway, I'd already decided there was no way I was going to stay in a stranger's house as part of their family, even though Miss did make the exchange sound like fun. But I knew for me the misery of sitting at a dinner table trying to make small talk with unfamiliar people, sharing someone else's bedroom, using someone else's bathroom, having someone else's mum doing my washing . . . yeek! . . . would far outweigh the fun to be had on all the excursions that we would go on.

I'm so pathetic. I've never even managed a sleepover yet and I'm nearly fourteen. To be honest, I've not tried for a year or two. The last time Mum had to come and rescue me at two o'clock in the morning from Fern's house because I had stomachache. I did, honest, I wasn't making it up.

What I didn't tell anyone though was, my stomach was hurting because I needed to go to the loo but I was holding it in because . . . well, I didn't want to go in Fern's bathroom. It's beautiful, all shiny mirrors and white marble tiles from floor to ceiling. It had a tall vase of fresh lilies by the loo and a white raffia chair beside the bath with big plump cushions. Next to it was a table with a selection of books on it. I never realized you could sit and read in bathrooms. Anyway, there was no way I could do my business in that perfect room, especially as, when I went to go in there, Fern's older brother, Duncan, was coming out of his bedroom too, but he stood back and said, 'After you.'

That was it. Constipation.

If I went on exchange, I wouldn't poo for a fortnight.

I find family life incredibly embarrassing. I mean, how do you manage living with so many other people? There is no privacy. The other day Fern's period started in school and she actually rang her dad up at work and asked him to get her some tampons on his way home. I went red just listening to her. And what was even worse, she did it in front of Adam, and he never turned a hair. He's got two sisters of his own; I suppose he's used to it. It's not a big deal for them.

It is for me though.

Actually, if I'm honest, I find life embarrassing, full stop. I guess mine's been pretty sheltered. There's just Mum and me, you see. No one else. My dad died when I was little; I can hardly remember him. Sometimes I worry that Mum will die too. If she's late home from work or sometimes in the middle of the night when I can't sleep, I think about what would happen to me if she dropped dead. I suppose I'd end up in care, with lots of other people. Which I'd hate.

Mum calls me her Little Stressling. She also calls me Wilma Worryguts, Tessie Tizzwizz and Minnie Mouse. I know she'd like me to lighten up and be more outgoing. *I'd* like me to lighten up and be more outgoing but it's easier said than done. The more I think about my shyness, the worse it gets.

The funny thing is, deep inside, I'm not shy at all. I mean, I don't think I've got low self-esteem or anything. I'm not boasting, but I know I'm not bad-looking, because boys are always trying to get off with me and Fern says if she had my straight fair hair and figure she'd flaunt it, no worries. I don't know what it is. On my own I'm a real show-off, like I'll sing and dance in front of the long mirror in Mum's wardrobe like nobody's business, but when there's anyone else around, I clam up. It's like an affliction.

Anyway, I crammed the letter into my bag and forgot all about it. Big mistake. Two days later my mother comes home from work and starts rooting through my bag.

'What are you doing?' I ask in alarm.

'Holly's mum tells me she's going on exchange,' says Mum. 'Ah, here it is.' She brandishes the letter in my face. 'Why didn't you say anything?'

'I don't want to go,' I say airily, like it's no big deal. Why hadn't I got rid of the incriminating evidence? 'It's boring.'

'Don't be silly,' scoffs Mum. 'It's a great opportunity.' She sifts through the information. 'It takes place over the Easter holidays!' she says, her voice rising in excitement.

My heart sinks. I know exactly where she's coming from. Mum only gets Friday and Monday off at Easter whereas the school holidays stretch to a fortnight. She hates leaving me on my own and pays old Mrs Bick from down the road to come in at holiday times even though there's no need. All she does is sit on the sofa, watching daytime soaps and stuffing her face with biscuits, and she pops home every hour, supposedly to check on her flea-bitten dog, but she comes back stinking of smoke so it's obvious she's been feeding her nicotine habit.

'It's really cheap!' Mum exclaims and I can see her precious tenners skipping merrily back out of Mrs Bick's hand and into the housekeeping. 'This would be such a good thing to do.'

'No it wouldn't, it would be horrible.'

'It's not just going to school, you know. They lay on trips for you. There's one to a castle and another to an art gallery,' she says, scanning the pages.

'I hate castles and art galleries,' I mutter, but it's not really true.

'They say there will be a festival on because it's Easter. They go in for them in a big way . . .'

'Big deal!' I say rudely, though this does sound interesting. What sort of festival? I wonder. Music? Dancing in the streets? Film or theatre? Mum carries on reading out the itinerary.

'. . . a visit to the mountains . . . a day at the seaside . . . a tour of the city, with time for shopping. How lovely!'

Mum beams at me.

I scowl at her.

The next minute she's crouching down beside me. 'What is it, Tizz Wizz?'

'Dunno.' I shrug my shoulders but she's not fooled.

'Holly's going,' she urges.

'So?' I know what she means without her saying it. Holly's mum and dad are in the middle of splitting up, but Holly's still brave enough to go on the exchange

'And Fern. She's going too.'

'I know she is.' She'd talked about nothing else for the past two days. 'Everyone's going,' I admit.

Mum sighs heavily. 'It would do wonders for your self-confidence, you know.' She tucks a stray wisp of hair behind my ears. 'Why don't you give it a go? I'm sure you'd like it if you tried.'

I meet her eyes. They're soft and pleading. Poor Mum. Why did she have to end up with a wuss like me? I knew how she fretted about leaving me on my own and I really did not want to spend a fortnight sitting on the sofa with Mrs Bick, watching her dunk biscuits into her tea and listening to her clearing her throat and sniffing every couple of minutes.

'You'd be picking up a bit of Spanish before you start your GCSEs next year,' she prompts.

That's true. And if I didn't go, everyone else would have a head start on me.

'Would I have to speak Spanish?'

'That's the general idea.'

'But I don't know any.'

'They know that. That's the reason you're going there, to learn the language. You'll pick it up quickly this way, spending time in the country, living with a nice little Spanish girl, going to school with her.'

She made it sound easy-peasy.

'You'll all be in the same boat,' she says encouragingly. 'Starting from scratch. No one will expect you to be able to say much.'

Just as well. I'd be struck dumb with embarrassment anyway.

But actually, it wouldn't matter, would it, if I was? They'd just think I didn't understand.

'They say they match you really carefully with your exchange partner,' says Mum quietly.

'How can they do that?'

'Well you could ask to be paired with someone like you.'

Someone like me? Who was that? Someone who hates attracting attention to herself, but paradoxically always manages to do so by her amazing ability to blush to the roots of her hair.

Actually, that might be quite nice for a change. I mean, Fern is great, but she's so super-confident she hasn't got a clue what it feels like to be me. 'I wish I had your figure!' she'd moan, failing to grasp how much I hated the attention my newly acquired boobs brought me. It would be good to make friends with someone else who preferred to shun the limelight. We could talk about what it felt like, once I'd learned enough Spanish. Then she could come over here and I could teach her English and show her around. We could be friends.

'An only child perhaps,' continues Mum. We're thinking on the same wavelength.

'Would I have to share a bedroom?'

'I wouldn't have thought so. You might even have an en-suite bathroom to yourself.'

'Do you reckon?' I say hopefully.

'I wouldn't be surprised. When I stayed in a Spanish villa on holiday, every bedroom had an en-suite. And that was years ago.'

'Really?'

'Look,' says Mum, pressing home her advantage, 'there's a section here for special requests. Why don't you put down exactly what you want?'

I hesitate for a second. It wouldn't do any harm would it, to make a list?

'OK then. But it doesn't mean I'm going to go,' I warn, just in case she thinks it's a done and dusted deal.

'Absolutely,' she says, but I notice she's already signing the parental consent form.

In the end, these are the things I wrote.

I want my exchange partner to:
1. *be female.*
2. *be an only child.*
3. *provide me with my own bedroom. (compulsory)*
4. *provide me with my own en-suite bathroom. (compulsory)*

10

5. have a single parent. (optional)
6. be looking for friendship.
7. be genuine, kind and caring.
8. like reading and watching romantic movies.

I wanted two more to make it ten, a nice round number. What I really wanted to write was *be as shy as me,* but that sounded pathetic. In fact, PANIC! My whole list sounded pathetic!

I mean, I did want to have fun on this trip *if* I did decide to go on it. I didn't want to end up with some sad loner just because I have a tendency to blush a bit.

OK. To blush a lot.

But that's not the point. I still like having a good time. So I added:

9. be fit and fun-loving.

Then suddenly I remembered those initials you always see in the personal columns of the newspaper and wrote:

10. have a GSOH.

There! That rounded it off nicely.

'What's a gussoh?' asks Mum, reading over my shoulder.

'A good sense of humour,' I explain. She laughs out loud.

'It reads like one of those dating adverts. You can't put that in.'

'Yes I can! You said I could put down exactly what I wanted. I don't want to stay with a boring old misery-guts.'

Mums know more than you think they do. I should have listened to her.

But I didn't.

That's how I ended up with Concha.

I should have realized when we turned up at the airport to find it fogbound and all the flights cancelled, that the trip was doomed from the start. Fifty-six hours later, having survived the ferry crossing from hell and a nightmare coach journey through France and Spain, tired, hungry, thirsty, fed up, feeling sick and honking to high heaven, we arrive at our Spanish destination in the middle of the night.

Fortunately the school, which is on the outskirts of the city, is ablaze with lights and a big throng of kids with their families is there to greet us. As the coach comes to a stop, a cheer goes up from the waiting crowd and we perk up.

'I wonder which one is Dolores?' says Fern, anxiously peering through the window as Miss Martínez and the other staff get out to meet the Spanish teachers. Dolores means 'pain'. I'm glad I'm not paired with her.

Spanish names are amazing. My exchange partner is called Concepción Inmaculada Gómez López. I kid you not. She lives in a three-bedroomed flat with her father who is a single parent. Each bedroom has an en-suite bathroom. I've got what I wanted. Miss Martínez says her name means 'The Immaculate Conception', and she's called after the mother of Jesus. *Her* name, because she's Spanish by the way, is Maria Martínez. It sounds loads better than plain old Mary Martin which is what it would be in English.

I was quite pleased when we got the information about who we'd been placed with. I mean someone who's named after the Virgin Mary is going to be nice, aren't they? I'm thinking kind, pretty, gentle, long-suffering . . . Better than someone called *Pain*! It was worth filling in the special request section. I bet Fern wishes she'd done it now.

Mr Evans, the PE teacher who'd come to look after the boys, clambers back on the bus clutching a clipboard. 'Right then,' he bellows, 'we made it, finally! Time to meet your host families. You'll soon be fed, watered and tucked up in bed!'

No one objects to being spoken to as if they're six years old. In fact, after that hideous journey we *feel* like we're six years old. I'm even too tired to be nervous. All I want to do is shower, crawl into a nice clean bed and sleep for a week.

We shamble out of the coach and line up obediently. We look a mess. I can feel the Spanish kids appraising us, silently and critically. One or two giggle but their parents hush them up. I'm past caring. One by one, Mr Evans calls out our names and a family steps forward to claim the lucky student. First Holly disappears with a thin, dark girl and her parents, then Adam goes off with a family of boys. Slowly the crowd disperses as they collect their guests. Fern is enfolded into the arms of Dolores's mum who plants a big kiss on both cheeks then pushes forward her daughter to do the same. Fern and Dolores laugh at each other and I'm jealous. I'm Fern's friend, Dolores, not you! She doesn't look a pain at all as she picks up Fern's bag; she looks really nice with long dark hair and a big, wide grin. Fern obviously thinks so too because she goes off happily with her without a backward glance.

When will it be my turn?

Soon, I'll be the only one left.

Problem. I *am* the only one left.

Literally.

There is no partner for me.

Miss Martínez and Mr Evans look surprised.

Then they look concerned.

The Spanish teachers shout at each other.

Then they pout their lips and shrug with their hands open wide.

Then they look resigned.

Cold, dank fear curls itself into the pit of my stomach.

The one in charge, who is called Señor something unpronounceable which sounds like Hairy Ears, starts jabbering away at top speed to Miss Martínez. She looks a bit alarmed and fires back an equally unintelligible rally of Spanish and for a while it sounds like machine-gunfire as they yell at each other. My teacher seems far more excitable here in Spain than she does at home. After a bit, Señor Hairy Ears takes his mobile out and shouts into it. His face clears and he prattles away at Miss again who seems relieved. She picks up my case and bungs it into the back of his little car.

'Señor Hairy Ears will take you to Concepción Inmaculada's house!' she explains, then bundles me in after it before I've got a chance to object. I turn round to look through the back window as we drive away. Miss Martínez is rubbing her brow, like she's got a headache.

I've got one too.

Soon I'm being driven at breakneck speed through the streets of the city, back the way we came. I'm hanging on to the door handle for grim death to prevent myself being swung from side to side and I haven't got a clue what is happening, even though Señor Hairy Ears tries to explain to me in minute detail. But his non-stop commentary is wasted because I have absolutely no idea what he's saying and the barrage of words are an assault on my poor exhausted brain. After a while I close my eyes, hoping that sleep will rescue me from this nightmare. Mercifully, he lapses into silence but I'm too tense to nod off.

After what seems like hours, the car finally slows down and comes to a halt. I risk taking a peek. We've pulled up in front of a block of flats and it's obvious we've reached our destination because Señor has leapt out of the car and is pressing a buzzer. After a while, he barks into a grille and the front door swings open. The next minute he's hustling me through it and into a lift. We've arrived.

When the lift door opens at the third floor, a man is waiting for us. He's about Mum's age, short, stocky and tanned, with well-groomed, shiny black hair, tinged with grey. He's got really smiley eyes and very white teeth and he's not bad-looking for a middle-aged guy. He looks like a businessman because he's wearing a well-cut suit and an open-necked shirt even though it's late at night, and his shoes are polished and shiny. He shakes Señor by the hand and then turns to me and does a little bow and shakes mine too. I'm glad he doesn't do that double kiss thing, especially when I smell tobacco on him.

'I am Señor Gómez. I am so sorry we were not there to meet you,' he says in perfect, very formal English with a heavy accent. 'We were expecting you two days ago. I am afraid Concha forgot to inform me of your new time of arrival.'

'Concha?'

'My daughter. Concepción Inmaculada. Concha for short. She arranged all this herself. She will be so pleased to see you. She is asleep now, I'm afraid.'

'That's all right. I just want to get to bed myself.'

He looks at me and says kindly, 'Yes, I am sure you must be exhausted after your long journey. Would you like something to eat first?'

'No thanks. Just bed.'

'Come in. Let me show you to your room.'

He picks up my case and we pass a room with ¡PRIVADO! on a piece of paper pinned to the door. 'Concha's!' he says, a little shamefaced, but I don't mind. I'm all for privacy, me. He shows me into another bedroom which has a huge bed with beautiful plump pillows and a lace bedspread. I sink on to it gratefully. The shower can wait till morning. As I get into bed I hear Señor Hairy Ears making his goodbyes, then the front door shuts and the lights go out.

I'm here at last.

* * *

In the morning I'm woken up by someone shouting. At first I haven't a clue where I am but as my eyes adjust to the gloom I see I am in a big room with a high ceiling, in the centre of which a large, rotating fan hums loudly. I didn't notice the sound last night, I must have been too zonked. It's dark in the room and at first I think there is no window, then I realize there is one, but it has shutters over it. The bed is so soft and comfortable I debate turning over and going back to sleep but a high female voice outside my bedroom door is shouting, no screeching now, in Spanish, and I can hear Señor Gómez's deeper tones soothing and hushing it up. There is a torrent of invective followed by a door banging, then all goes quiet.

It must be the maid. Miss Martínez said that some Spanish homes have hired help, especially if the mother works. Poor Concha doesn't have a mother.

I can't wait to meet her. I sweep back the bedspread and run over to the window to open the shutters. They fold back to reveal a full-length window and a tiny verandah protected by a waist-high, wrought-iron balustrade. I open the window and step out on to the balcony. The morning sun is already hot on my face. Beneath me is a courtyard and through the canopy of vines and brightly-coloured flowers I can see a big wooden table and chairs set for breakfast. It looks beautiful, like a picture from a travel brochure.

I turn back to examine the room, now the morning light is flooding into it. It gives the impression of space and coolness. The walls are whitewashed and the floor is made up of deep red tiles scattered with patterned rugs, and is cool beneath my feet. There is a big, heavy wardrobe, so dark it almost looks black, with two drawers beneath it. On one wall is a large wooden crucifix and a big framed photo of a family, handsome father, pretty mother and a little girl dressed in white, all smiling into the camera. On the other, are two holy pictures: one I think is a picture of Christ with a bleeding heart and the other is of the Virgin Mary. That's it. Nothing else.

I sigh with satisfaction. It's just like I expected. Really Spanish. I pick up my wash bag and go to investigate the en-suite.

It's perfect. Modern, which is just what a bathroom should be, though actually, there is no bath. No need. Instead there's a brilliant power shower which is easy to operate and fiercely efficient, blasting away with almost painful force the last dregs of that horrible journey. Afterwards, feeling clean and refreshed, I wrap a small towel round my hair like a turban and swathe myself in a huge luxury white towel. I'm going to like it here.

Back in the bedroom I select a new outfit – cut-off blue jeans and a pink T-shirt – dress quickly, then start to unpack. When I open the double doors of the wardrobe, I have a surprise. A row of clothes is hanging soberly on the rail. They are all very similar, dark, restrained and severe, dresses, skirts and blouses which obviously belong to an older person. Feeling a bit awkward I push them over to one side and hang my things beside them. When I investigate further I find one of the drawers contains a collection of undergarments that are definitely old-woman, the impression heightened by the faint smell of lavender. I stare at the boned corsets and long-legged knickers in awe and suppress the urge to giggle, then slam it shut and fold my stuff in neat piles into the one below, marvelling how two sets of female underwear could be so completely different.

Everything in its place. I like that. Now for my hair. I look around for a hairdryer but there doesn't seem to be one. Time to brave the outside world, Jaime, you can do this.

I open the door and peer out cautiously. Across from me I spot the notice '¡PRIVADO!' on Concha's door and smile to myself. I know how she feels, I like my privacy too. Thank goodness I don't have to share a bedroom. At the end of the corridor I see the kitchen through an open door and I can hear the rattle of crockery and smell the delicious aroma of proper roasting coffee. The maid must be preparing breakfast. From the sound of her screeching this morning I don't think I'm ready to brave her yet. Instead I tiptoe across to Concha's bedroom and take a deep breath. Then I knock tentatively on the door, three soft little raps.

There's no answer. I do it again, a little louder this time. From inside I think I can hear somebody moving about but no one comes to the door. I try once more, seven raps this time in a jolly little rhythm, two slow, three fast, two slow, *duh, duh, de-duh-duh, duh, duh,* and rest my ear against the door, trying to listen for movement inside. The door opens and I stumble, grabbing the door frame to keep my balance.

'What do you want?' asks a clear, clipped voice. A girl stands before me scowling, her hands on her hips. She is short with thick black hair that comes to just beneath her ears and heavy eyebrows which are drawn together in a deep frown, so it looks as if she has one angry line across her brow.

'Um . . . I'm looking for a hair dryer,' I answer. 'I'm Jaime.'

'I know that,' she says. 'I'm not stupid.'

'You must be Concha?' I say, totally flustered.

'Give the girl a prize,' she says in a bored voice. Her eyebrows separate into two and rise disdainfully as she studies me. 'Why have you gone red?'

Two things register in my befuddled brain.

Number one: her English is perfect, with hardly a trace of an accent.

Number two: I hate her.

'Do you have a hairdryer I could borrow?' I repeat, surprising myself with my persistence, but I need one otherwise my hair dries all over the place and anyway, I don't know what else to say.

She turns away as if she's ignoring me but the next second she's back, thrusting a hairdryer into my hand. 'Be my guest,' she says in the same bored tone.

'Thanks.'

She appraises me coolly. 'I thought you were a boy, you know. That's the only reason I agreed to have you here. Well, that and I wanted to go to the UK. I've changed my mind now.'

'Why did you think I was a boy?' I ask in surprise.

'Duh!' she says rudely. 'Your name? Jaime?'

'Oh.' She glares at me as if I owe her some kind of explanation. 'It's spelt differently, though. If I was a boy it would be spelt J A M I E.'

'Not in Spain, it wouldn't. J A I M E is the Spanish for James.'

'Sorry,' I say meekly, then wonder why I'm apologizing to this girl for my own name. She hasn't finished yet.

'And your special requests,' she continues, her tone accusatory. 'What was all that about?'

'What?'

'You said you wanted a female for friendship and fun. Must be fit. Looking for romance, you said.'

'No I didn't!' I deny hotly, at the same time racking my brain trying to remember exactly what I did write down.

'Yes you did! Good sense of humour, you wrote. That's what people always put when they're looking for a relationship! You deliberately misled me!'

I close my eyes. I should have listened to Mum. 'Sorry,' I repeat. 'I didn't mean to.'

'Now I'm stuck with you for a fortnight,' she grumbles. 'And what's even worse, Abuela's coming to stay as well now and it's all your fault.'

'How come?' I say, indignation rising. She can't blame me for that, surely? I've never even met Abuela, whoever that is.

'She insists. She says it's not right for a young foreign girl to be staying unaccompanied in a flat without a woman in charge. She's arriving today. Don't bother to unpack.'

'Why not?'

'Because you haven't got a bedroom any more!'

Then she slams the door shut in my face.

Señor Gómez is nice. It was him in the kitchen, not the maid. Probably there is no maid. I've worked it out. Concha was the person doing all the screeching, presumably after her father had informed her that I'd made it here after all. I think she was hoping if she didn't tell him he had to meet me last night, then I'd simply disappear. Once she'd discovered I wasn't a boy, she'd changed her mind about having an exchange partner.

'*Buenos días!*' he says cheerily, rescuing me from the corridor where I'm standing like an idiot gazing open-mouthed at Concha's closed door. He sits me down at the kitchen table and gives me breakfast. It's a bit weird. He hands me a big bowl of coffee, without a handle or anything, and indicates a plate of cakes.

'Help yourself.'

I didn't need any more bidding, I was starving. More of an afternoon tea than a breakfast but who cares? But the coffee is bitter and far too strong for me and the cake is terribly, chokingly, dry and sweet. Then I notice that Señor Gómez has chucked his cakes into his coffee and is sort of slurping them down. I follow suit and dunk my cake in the coffee too and discover they're not quite so bad this way. My mother would have a fit if she could see what I was doing.

But she's not here, is she? All of a sudden I have trouble swallowing and it's got nothing to do with my peculiar breakfast.

I miss my mum.

How am I going to get through the next two weeks?

'I hope you will be happy here,' says Señor Gómez doubtfully, as if he's reading my mind. 'I am sure you will have fun with Concha.'

I meet his eyes and he looks away quickly. We continue to gulp down our sloppy breakfast in silence. There is nothing else to say. After a while he stands up and puts on his jacket which is on the back of the chair.

'Work!' he announces. 'Concha will look after you.'

Like we both know that's going to happen!

'Where am I sleeping?' I ask.

'With Concha,' he says firmly. He raps on her door and says something to her in Spanish. In return, a barrage of cursing in both English and Spanish bursts through the closed door. Bilingual abuse, obviously directed at

26

me. Scary but impressive. Imagine being able to swear in two languages!

Señor Gómez turns to me. 'She says, whenever you are ready you may move your things into her room,' he says courteously.

Yeah, right!

I wait to see what he does next. After a while he clears his throat, then studies his watch.

'Is that the time?' he says gratefully and springs into action. 'I am late!'

'*Adiós*,' I say, trying out my first word of Spanish. That's why I'm here after all.

'*¡Adiós!*' he answers and beams at me in delight, grateful I suppose that I haven't actually run away screaming yet from this madhouse. Not that I'm not considering it. 'Have a nice day,' he adds and does a funny little clicky thing with his heels then he disappears out of the door. Fast. Two minutes later, in the street below, I hear a car revving up, then screeching away.

Silence falls.

I'm left on my own with Scary Mad Girl.

I sit there as still as can be, afraid to move, watching the blue cloudless sky through the window. From the street below I can hear cars hooting and people's voices as they make their way to work. Though no sound comes from her bedroom, I am aware of Concha on the other side of the closed door, listening, like a cat ready to pounce if I make a move on her territory. The walls of the kitchen are whitewashed like the bedroom but their blank canvas is broken up by pretty blue mosaic tiles and a large clock that ticks down the seconds.

One, two, three, four . . . five hundred and ninety-eight, five hundred and ninety-nine, six hundred. Ten minutes, I've sat here, mesmerized, counting down the seconds.

'You'll have the time of your life,' Mum had said, the night before we left, when I'd got the butterflies. Well, no, actually, Mum, what I want to say to you is, 'This is *wasting* my life.' It's worse than sitting on the sofa with Mrs Bick. I get up, suddenly angry, and stalk into my room . . . Abuela's room . . . to look for my itinerary. I didn't go through that awful coach trip across France and Spain for the best part of three days just to sit here alone in some strange kitchen. Correction. Some strange person's kitchen.

I find it in my bag but first I have to work out what day it is. It must be Thursday by now. We've missed a day at school and a day at the castle. Today we should be at school again. Tomorrow is Good Friday and there is a festival.

School. When I was at home the thought of going to

a Spanish school terrified me. Now anything seems preferable to spending time alone with Crazy Girl. At least Fern would be there! Fired with determination, I march back up to Concha's door and knock loudly and this time I don't wait to be invited in, I open the door myself.

'Yes?' she says, icily. She's sitting on the floor, cross-legged, her hair covering her face. It smells of honey. In her hand is a pair of hair straighteners. She's still in her pyjamas.

'Shouldn't we be going to school?' I ask, my eyes sweeping over the room, with its scattered clothes and used mugs and plates, then coming back to rest on the mop of black hair. It's hard talking to someone with hair covering their face. It's like having a conversation with the back of someone's head.

She sweeps her hair back and examines herself critically in a small mirror perched on top of a pile of books. 'Yes,' she repeats. On the floor beside her is a piece of paper with a name repeated over and over again in large black letters. Pablo . . . Pablo . . . Pablo. In between each line is a row of red hearts with the words 'Concha4Pablo' printed neatly between them. Wow, she's got it bad. She obviously wants to impress this Pablo. I wait patiently while she outlines her eyes with kohl then expertly adds mascara to her upper and lower lashes, which I have to admit, are pretty impressive even without make-up. When she's finished, her eyes look huge but hard.

My school would go ballistic if I turned up in that amount of make-up. Spanish schools must be more casual.

'Are we going then?' I ask.

'When I'm ready.' She adds a touch of blusher and some lip-gloss and then jumps up and starts sifting through her wardrobe. After a minute, she chooses a black skirt and a white shirt and starts dressing. I wonder whether I should leave the room but she doesn't seem bothered. Her body is short and sturdy, with toned muscles. The skirt is knee-length but she doubles the waistband back over itself till it rests just below her bum. I recognize what she is doing; I've used that trick myself, to make my legs look longer, but not to go to school!

I glance down at my cut-off jeans.

'Am I OK like this?' I ask. She gives me a sideways look, and shrugs.

'Suppose so,' she says.

'Where did you learn to speak like that?' I ask, my curiosity getting the better of me.

'Like what?'

'You're so fluent. Anyone would think you were English.'

'The States,' she says, momentarily looking pleased, as

if I'd paid her a compliment, which I suppose I had. Not that I wanted to. Then she adds in her normal, surly tone, like she's suddenly remembered she's meant to be unpleasant, 'if you must know.'

'Did you live there?' I ask, determined not to be put off.

'Yes.'

'How long?'

'Three years.'

'Who with? Your dad?'

'My mother.' For a second, her voice sounds wistful and her face is sad. Questions race through my brain, elbowing each other out of the way.

When did you live there?

Why aren't you living there any more?

Where's your mother now?

Is she dead?

I open my mouth but Concha glares at me and I close it again. Perhaps not.

'What is this?' she asks in a steely voice. 'The third degree?'

'No,' I say, surprising myself with my own attempt at wit. 'It's an inquisition. The Spanish Inquisition!'

A fleeting expression passes across Concha's face, lightening the brooding brow, softening the hard eyes, turning up the edges of the down turned mouth. For a

31

second, she looks almost pretty.

Then it's gone, so quickly I think I must have imagined it.

'Have you got a boyfriend?' she asks suddenly.

'No. Have you?'

'Not at the moment. But there is someone I like.'

'What's his name?' I ask, just to show a bit of interest, being as she's finally opening up to me, though it's blatantly obvious it's this Pablo whose name she has scrawled everywhere.

She hesitates. Then she says sharply, 'Mind your own business,' and the door clangs shut again. She picks up her bag. 'Come on, I don't want to be late.'

I don't object. I don't tell her that it's her fault if we are, *I've* been waiting for ages. I just grab my bag and follow her out of the apartment.

It's enough for now.

I made her smile.

And she nearly confided in me.

Outside it's already hot. 'We have to get a bus,' remarks Concha, so I get my wallet out and examine my euros while we wait. Concha pulls out some gum, stuffs it into her mouth without offering me any, and stares blankly into the distance, chewing open-mouthed. I think she's forgotten all about me. The euros look like toy money. 'How much is the fare?' I ask as the bus pulls up.

Concha hands me a pass and says, 'Show it to the driver.'

I do as I'm told then follow her to the back of the bus and gaze out of the window as we drive through the busy streets. The buildings are tall, blocking out the sun, with shops on the lower floors and offices above. Most of the shops are still shuttered but there are hundreds of people on the streets, walking briskly to work, pouring out of buses, many of them carrying steaming cardboard cups of coffee. Most are smartly dressed, the women with short, neat hair and well-cut clothes, the men in business suits, like Señor Gómez.

After a while the bus leaves the city behind and trundles its way into the suburbs which are full of huge, concrete blocks of flats and bare patches of waste ground. A few more kids in school uniform start to get on the bus, but they sit at the front and nobody greets Concha. Two girls get on together, about our age, both of them dark, long-legged, pretty. They sound nice, giggling and chatting away to each other excitedly in fast Spanish voices as they make their way up the aisle towards us, and my heart lifts. Perhaps not all Spanish kids are as moody as Concha. But then they look up and spot us and fall silent, taking up seats in the middle of the bus.

Concha spits something out in Spanish and I know

1. it's not nice and

2. they've heard what she said.

I can tell by the way they sit there, steadfastly ignoring us, their backs stiff and tense. One girl mutters something under her breath and the other one laughs wryly and turns it quickly into a cough. I risk a quick peek at Concha. She's scowling, her brows drawn together again in what has already become a familiar black line.

'Slappers!' she translates loudly into English. 'They think they are babes but really they are tarts!'

I sit there, frozen to the spot, hoping against hope that the girls' English is not up to Concha's standard. She continues to grumble aloud. 'Look at the effort they make just to go to school! They won't be seen dead in public without a full makeover. Pathetic!'

My mind flips back to a picture of Concha earlier on, straightening her hair with fierce concentration, meticulously applying eyeliner, mascara, blusher, lip-gloss, raising the waistline of her skirt. Wisely I refrain from pointing this out. Apart from risking her wrath I don't want the girls to think I'm discussing them, so I sit there mute as Concha rants on, in a mixture of Spanish and English. More kids get on, greeting each other, but no one approaches us. I don't blame them.

After a while my curiosity gets the better of me.

'Why do you travel such a long way to school?' I ask just as the bus pulls into a lay-by beside a high wire fence. Beyond it is a yard with hundreds of kids swarming around and I recognize the school from last night. Everyone piles off the bus. Concha stands up without a word, sweeping back her hair.

'Isn't there a school nearer your home?' I continue, annoyed that she chooses to ignore me whenever she feels like it.

'Of course there is, stupid,' she says. My cheeks blaze, but oddly her rudeness makes me more persistent.

'So why don't you go there then?'

Her eyes roll up to her hairline.

'Because I got chucked out,' she says and swings her bag up on to her shoulders. The corner of it catches my shoulder and knocks me off balance, back on to the seat.

'Come on!' she says. 'You can't sit there all day.'

I grab my bag and follow her off the bus, wishing I could die, wishing she would die, wishing there was some way I could teleport myself back home. Trust me to be paired up for a fortnight with a nutter.

But then, amongst the black and white uniform in the yard, I spot Fern's new outfit, bought especially for the trip, a bright green dress with a figure-hugging belt, and there she is with the lovely Dolores. Fern sees me and her face breaks into a huge smile and she waves like mad. Immediately I feel better.

I look for Concha but she's striding ahead of me without a backward glance across the yard, assuming, I suppose, that I'll be following her like the sheep she thinks I am. Her skirt has ridden up so high her knickers are showing and people are nudging each other and laughing. I turn away, feeling better still, and make my way over to Fern.

'This is my best friend, Jaime,' she says to Dolores and I fall into Fern's arms with relief. Dolores gives me a friendly smile. We start chatting away together in broken English and I discover to my relief that not all Spanish girls are weirdos.

'Who is your exchange partner?' she asks.

'Concha!' I say and she shudders and says something I think I heard Concha shouting at her dad earlier on.

Then she says firmly, 'Concha, bad girl. You stay with me,' and links her arm through mine. When the bell goes, the three of us make our way into school together and Dolores takes us to our classroom.

Inside, everyone is milling around, laughing and chatting. Only Concha sits on her own at the back of the classroom, an expression of disdain on her face. When the teacher walks into the room everyone moves to their seats, taking their exchange partner with them. Everyone except me, that is. I stand there, uncertain what to do.

'Sit here!' hisses Fern, and Dolores grabs me by the arm and pushes me down into the chair next to hers. The teacher goes to object, then her eyes move to Concha then back to me and she hesitates.

'Where would you like to sit?' she asks me.

I can feel everyone's eyes upon me. This is my own worst nightmare. My cheeks start to burn as I turn to look at Concha, expecting her to say something cutting like, 'I don't want *her* sitting by me!'

Instead, she's staring out of the window, her chin on her hand, making out that she's bored to tears and doesn't care where the hell I sit. But then, suddenly, I notice a tiny spot of colour high on *her* cheeks which I've never seen before and it's definitely not the blusher she put on earlier. Most people wouldn't even notice it but I do. Suddenly I know that she does care, actually, she cares very much indeed.

'I'll sit by Concha,' I say and get up and move quietly to the back of the classroom to join her.

Concha is SCARY!

First lesson she swears at the teacher and gets sent out of class. Only she refuses to go. I think that's what happened. I'm not absolutely sure because it's all in Spanish, but the teacher is definitely having a go at her about something, her make-up I think, and suddenly Concha shrieks out this word and everyone gasps. The teacher yells at her and points at the door but she won't budge. Instead she screams back at the teacher and points at me! At first I think she's blaming me for whatever she's done, then I work out she's saying she has to stay and look after me. The teacher gives *me* a stinking look anyway as if it's all my fault, but Concha gets her way and stays put!

Then, at breaktime, she links her arm through mine and marches me off with her. I have no idea where we are going, it feels more like she's taking me prisoner than being friendly. I don't want to go, I want to stay with Fern and Dolores, but I have no choice. She takes me behind this big shed and produces a cigarette and a match from down her sock, sparks up, takes a big drag, blows two (impressive!) smoke rings, then offers it to me. I shake my head and she says, 'Go on!' encouragingly, like she thinks I'm just being polite.

'I don't smoke,' I explain and she looks disappointed, then her lip curls.

'Little Miss Goody-Goody,' she sneers and takes another drag, blowing the smoke disdainfully into my face.

'No I'm not!' I say angrily, trying not to cough. 'I just don't like smelling like an old ash tray.'

Her eyes narrow and my heart sinks. But then, thank goodness, a familiar face appears around the corner of the shed and distracts her. It's Adam, and though at home he's the one who gets us into trouble, he's a pussy compared to wild-cat Concha and I'm so pleased to see him.

'Jaime?' he says in surprise. 'What are you doing in the smokers' den?' With him is a dark, curly-haired boy with a round, open face and cheeky grin. When he spots Concha he stops short as if he's changed his mind and his smile fades, but Adam hands him a fag and he decides to stay.

'This is Ignacio,' explains Adam, lighting up. 'That's a mouthful, innit?'

'Nacho,' says the boy in halting English. 'You can call me Nacho.'

'Ain't that food?' asks Adam, looking bewildered. 'I'm sure I've eaten nachos at home.'

'Adam . . . exchange . . . no . . . *intercambio* . . . *amigo* . . . Nacho?' I ask hesitantly.

'*Sí!*' he beams, his face almost splitting into two.

'Jaime's dead clever!' says Adam. 'She's picking up the lingo already.'

I smile modestly. Next to me Concha snorts.

I don't care. This Spanish malarkey is easier than I thought. Mum was right. I don't feel quite so shy out here, with a different language. It's like people aren't judging you on *what* you say, it's more on *how much* you can say. And I'm a quick learner.

Two older boys appear, they look like sixth-formers. Nacho drops the cigarette from his fingers but it's too late, he's been spotted. Prefects? I notice Adam has cupped his inside his palm and I wonder uneasily if we are going to get into trouble but Concha makes no attempt to hide her cigarette. Instead her face lights up and she beams at the newcomers.

'Hey, Eduardo!' she cries and high-fives the taller guy. The other one yells at Nacho and cuffs him on the side of his head and Nacho drops the cigarette and runs off, nursing his ear and shouting a torrent of Spanish abuse. The two boys and Concha laugh and Eduardo picks up the cigarette from the ground and puffs it back into life. Adam relaxes and takes a drag of his fag too. I study the newcomers. The shorter one has the same black, curly hair as Nacho but he's older, with a dark tinge to his cheeks, like he needs to shave every day. The penny drops.

'Is Ignacio your brother?' I ask.

'*Sí.*' He looks at me with interest. 'You speak Spanish?'

'Only a little.'

'*Un poco.*' he corrects and I repeat, '*Un poco,*' after him.

'*Perfecto,*' he says and smiles at me approvingly. 'You learn fast.'

I smile back at him. 'Thanks.'

This time his eyes take in the whole of me as if he likes what he sees. I can't believe I'm flirting like this. From the corner of my eye I can see Adam watching me in surprise.

Concha is watching me too. I can feel her eyes boring into me like red-hot probes.

'How do you do?' Suddenly he stretches out his hand and clicks his heels. 'Is that what you say in English?'

I shake his hand and giggle. 'It's a bit formal.'

'Formal?'

'Correct.' He looks confused. 'Too serious,' I explain, trying to let go of his hand, but his grip tightens and he pulls me towards him.

'Then we do it the Spanish way.' To my shock he plants a kiss lightly on each cheek. '*Encantado. Soy Pablo*,' he says. My face flares up immediately. I don't know where to look.

From a distance I hear a bell ringing and the sound of protest as a wave of people start making their way noisily back into school. Me, I can't move, stuck here out of my depth, face burning up, desperately treading water. Are all Spanish boys like this?

'He said, "*Pleased to meet you. I am Pablo.*"' Concha's voice is harsh but I turn to her anyway, grateful for the lifeline she is throwing me. But something is wrong. She's glaring at me so hard I feel as if she'd stab me with a boat-hook rather than come to my rescue. Now I really do feel as if I'm drowning. What have I done?

PABLO! My heart misses a beat. I get it. The boy who kissed me is *the* Pablo, the Pablo4Concha printed again and again across a row of identical red hearts, the Pablo who is the object of my exchange partner's affections. If she *has* any feelings that is, beneath that cold, hard-nosed exterior.

I wonder if he knows he's wearing one of her famous ¡PRIVADO! signs around his neck? Something tells me he's completely unaware of her interest in him. That something being the way he's looking at me now.

'The bell's gone!' I say abruptly. 'Come on, Adam.'

Adam, startled by me taking the lead, steps on his cigarette and follows me obediently. I stride out, desperate to get back into school and away from potential problems. The last thing I want to do is upset Concha. But just as I reach the steps into school, Pablo catches up with me and takes my arm, bringing me to a halt.

'I think you are a good teacher,' he remarks, treating me to a full-on smile. He has the most perfect teeth. 'You will have to give me lessons. I would like to study English one day at university.'

I glance behind me nervously just as Concha stalks past us and up the steps, eyes blazing, head held high.

'I don't know . . .'

'Please.' His smile fades and his tone alters, becoming less assertive, less sure. 'I would like to know you better, to speak English with you. Is that so bad?' His eyes search mine gravely. They are dark, almost black, their depths concealed by long, sweeping lashes, and the expression in them is pleading. You could drown in those eyes.

'No.'

'Good. Then we will meet again,' he says. 'I must go. Excuse me.'

Wow! What are Spanish boys like? A weird mixture of old-fashioned courtesy and full-on cockiness apparently. Or maybe that's just Pablo. What is he? Mr Manners or Mr Mean? Señor Nice or Señor Nasty?

I watch as he goes into school in front of me. He's not that tall, but he has broad shoulders and a muscular body like he works out, and he holds himself very straight, with just a suggestion of a slight swagger in the way he walks. Eduardo catches up with him at the door and they tussle, play-fighting their way through. He's forgotten me already, I think regretfully. Perhaps it's just as well. Then just before the door closes behind him he turns and winks at me.

'*Encantado*,' I whisper.

I've never met anyone like him in my life.

When I go back into class, my bag which I had left on my desk is lying on the floor, its contents strewn across the aisle. Dolores and Fern are picking them up for me. Concha is staring out of the window like she hasn't got a care in the world, but you can feel the tension in the classroom. People are staring at her like she's a firework waiting to go off.

'She just scattered your bag on to the floor when she came in from break,' says Fern indignantly when I bend down beside her. 'Cheek!'

Dolores shakes her head warningly and whispers, 'She is angry. Be careful.'

The teacher comes into the room and I stuff the rest of my things into my bag and slip into my seat beside Concha. She ignores me, thank goodness, and the lesson begins. It's geography and maybe because she's got all these exchange kids in her class, the teacher has planned a lesson on the British Isles. She gives out a set of atlases, but there are not quite enough to go around. The desks are old-fashioned individual ones, but she gets us to push them together so we can share. Concha looks at me like I'm a leper as I edge my desk closer to hers, and sticks her foot out to maintain a gap between us. Then she grabs the atlas and opens it up on her desk, turning her back to me so I can't see it.

I don't care if she wants to be childish, I'd rather concentrate on what the teacher is saying anyway and see what I can pick up.

But Señora Whatsername has a sense of justice. When she notices that Concha is hogging the atlas to herself she tells her off and Concha begrudgingly shifts the atlas closer towards me. I try to follow the lesson but it's difficult with Concha seething beside me. Before long the atlas has found its way back on to her desk.

Señora is a tough cookie. She spots what Concha has done and barks out a reproof in rapid Spanish and Concha swears under her breath and thrusts it back at me again. It folds up and disappears down the gap between the desks and everyone laughs. The teacher says the same word that Concha said under her breath and strides up to us and shoves my desk closer to Concha's. My exchange partner lets out a yell of pain. I can see her foot is jammed between the two desks, but the teacher doesn't notice. She bends down to pick up the atlas from the floor and slaps it down between us, knocking Concha on the head with it by accident. Concha howls in protest and shoves the atlas off the desk on to the teacher's toes. The teacher chucks her out of class.

After that the lesson progresses relatively smoothly though my insides have turned to slush.

At lunchtime Concha is nowhere to be seen. Some kids, those within walking distance, disappear home with their partners for lunch. The rest of us make our way to a covered picnic area with big wooden tables and benches, protected from the hot sun by a striped awning. I sit down next to Fern and Dolores who pull out bottles of drink and two large brown paper packets which they unwrap to reveal a fabulous array of breads, meats, cheeses and olives. My mouth waters.

'Where's yours?' asks Fern.

'I haven't got any.'

Dolores raps out something about Concha in Spanish which doesn't sound very nice and lots of the Spanish kids look horrified. Then everyone starts to jabber away in broken English and thrust food at me.

'Please!'

'I have much.'

'You want?'

'My mother! Too much!' This one is from Nacho and

is accompanied by much puffing out of his cheeks and patting of his belly which makes everyone laugh.

Soon I am surrounded by ripe furry peaches, fresh figs, bunches of juicy black grapes, dainty little cakes and a mountain of bread, meat and cheese.

'What's this?' asks Adam, staring at some fleshy meat covered in sauce in a plastic container which is part of his packed lunch.

'*Tripas*,' explains Nacho. 'Spanish delicacy. My mother made it especially for you.'

'*Tripas?*' Adam nibbled away experimentally. 'What's *tripas?*'

'Tripe?' Fern suggests.

'What's tripe?' repeats Adam, bemused, and Holly says, 'It's the stomach of a cow.'

'I thought it was a pig's intestines,' I say and then Jason suggests it's a pig's something else that's a bit more disgusting and Adam pulls a face and spits it out. All the English kids laugh and the Spanish kids want to know what is going on and so we have to try and explain to them, which is hilarious, then they fall about laughing too. But then Adam says, 'Actually, it's quite nice, try some,' and it is. So then we decide to put everything that people have brought for lunch in the middle of the table and we'll share it, just like a birthday party, and it's delicious and much more fun than just eating your own food. Definitely more fun in my case, because I didn't have any.

And I'm sitting there having a good time and marvelling quietly to myself how nice everyone is and how easy it is to get on with people who speak a different language and how I've just joined in a conversation about a pig's rude bits and I didn't even go red and how glad I am that I came on this trip when suddenly I spot Concha. She's standing at the top of the entrance steps with a teacher and she's looking really sullen. He points over to us and shouts out something to her in Spanish and she flounces down the steps and makes her way sulkily towards us.

'The headmaster,' explains Nacho, whose English seems better than everyone else's. Maybe, like his gorgeous brother, he's planning to study English at university. 'He says she must eat lunch with you and then return to his office this afternoon.'

I shift up uneasily to make room for Concha as she approaches but she stops short and glares at everyone, her hands on her hips. The table falls silent.

'Want some?' I offer. Concha's eyes widen as she takes in the spread on the table. No one else says a thing. The Spanish kids don't even look at her. It's obvious they don't want her to sit down. Her lip curls in a way that's becoming familiar.

'Let's get out of here,' she says to me. 'Go and find some decent food. I can't eat this crap.'

She is so rude! Fern and Holly gasp. Even Adam and Jason look embarrassed. I can feel my colour rising. 'You go,' I say. 'I'm fine.'

Concha pulls some notes out of her pocket. 'Come on,' she says. 'My dad gave me money for us both for lunch. We'll get some chicken and fries. Or pizza. Do you like pizza?'

Her voice falters. I gaze up at her. She looks a bit desperate, like she doesn't know what to do if I say no. I don't know what to do either. I don't want to upset her, I know enough about her already to see that would be a big mistake. But I can't get up and leave the table now, not after everyone's been so kind, sharing their food with me. I shake my head regretfully.

'Thanks, Concha. But I want to stay.'

She stares at me in surprise then unleashes a torrent of abuse in English at me. Even Holly, who has a reputation herself for being a bit of a foul mouth, looks shell-shocked. Finally she runs out of steam, stands still for a minute looking furious, stamps her foot and makes a sort of strangled sound in her throat and marches off out of the school gates. Immediately, everyone starts talking again.

'What a cow!' breathes Holly.

'Good for you, Jaime, for standing up to her,' says Fern.

'Concha is trouble,' warns Dolores.

Fern looks worried. 'Maybe you shouldn't get on the wrong side of her, Jaime.'

'I think it's a bit late for that,' I say forlornly. 'Anyway, I don't think she's got a good side, has she?'

Concha doesn't come back to school that afternoon. The rest of the day passes peacefully. After lunch, which was really long, we have English (easy-peasy, of course) and basketball, which is fun. I'm the shooter for the netball team at home so I'm good, and the Spanish kids pick up on this quickly. They shout instructions at me all the time and I quickly pick up some new words, like *'¡Rápido!'* which is obvious and *'¡Tira!'* which means 'Shoot!' It feels like my name in the end, they shout it so much.

At the end of school I have a problem. I need to get back to the flat but I'm not sure of the right bus to catch. Concha is nowhere to be seen and no one seems to know where she lives.

'Hasn't anyone ever been to her home?' I ask Dolores.

Her eyebrows go one way, her jaw the other. 'Concha's home?' She shudders.

'Her dad's nice,' I say, but she shakes her head in disbelief.

'What are you going to do?' asks Fern, concerned.

She knows what I'm like.

'I don't know.' I shrug my shoulders, like I don't care, but inside I'm starting to fret. It's been a good day, better than I expected, but it's been tiring. Now, all I want to do is go home, have a shower, have something to eat and chill out.

Instead of which I've got to work out how to get home.

THEN I've got to face Crazy Concha and the mysterious Abuela, whoever she is; even Concha seems in awe of her so she must be seriously scary.

AND I haven't got a bedroom to sleep in tonight.

AND Concha's going to hate me because I didn't go for lunch with her.

AND I never wanted to come on exchange in the first place.

AND NOW IT'S SUDDENLY ALL TOO MUCH!!

I'd been really proud of the way I'd handled everything so far. But now Wilma Worryguts is back with a vengeance. I can feel a lump in my throat forming and tears welling up.

'Let's go and ask Miss Martínez,' says Fern gently. I nod, hoping the tears won't spill, then suddenly I spot two girls boarding one of the buses drawn up outside the school. I recognize them immediately: they're the pretty ones Concha slagged off on the bus on the way to school this morning. They're going my way!

'It's OK, I can manage!' I say and without more ado I make a dash for the bus, squeezing through the doors just before they close. It's even the same driver! I flash my card at him and make my way to the back, and as I sit down I see Fern's surprised face through the window. I wave to her happily, feeling decisive and back in control.

I didn't know I could move that fast! Well, I am a shooter, after all! I'm not Wilma Worryguts any more. Tira has taken her place!

Tira! I giggle to myself. What am I like? I've reinvented myself as a character called Shoot. Come to think of it, it's a good name to have because to shoot means to pass quickly through time and space. Well, I can do that. I can be Tira while I'm in Spain, then I can speed through time and before I know it Crazy Concha will be nothing but a distant memory and I'll be safely back home again.

Tira.

She's strong.

She's fast.

She's tough.

I like her.

Tira gets me off the bus at the right stop, keeps me calm while I find my bearings then leads me back to the building where the Gómezes live. When I step out of the lift I can hear a babble of voices coming from their flat. I take a deep breath and square my shoulders before I rap loudly on the door. The voices cease then the door opens to reveal Concha, her face falling into its familiar scowl when she sees it's me, and for a second I think she's going to close the door on me.

But then Concha is pushed aside and an arm comes out and pulls me into the flat. I'm aware of a blur of black clothes, papery-thin skin, bright red lipstick and grey piled-up hair as my head is clasped tight between a pair of vice-like, blue-veined hands and turned from side to side. Kisses rain down on my cheeks. This is the second time I've been kissed today, but this experience is very different from the first because:

1. It's much more energetic.
2. I can feel tiny whiskery hairs tickling my cheeks.
3. There is a strong smell of lavender.
4. It's accompanied by a great number of Spanish words and expressions of endearment (I think) expressed in a hoarse, throaty voice.
5. I'm pretty sure it leaves me with bright red lipstick all over my face, because suddenly a white lace handkerchief is produced and my cheeks are scrubbed so hard I'm afraid the skin is going to come off and there's red all over the hanky and I don't *think* it's blood.

I think I've just met Abuela.

It turns out that *Abuela* is Spanish for Grandmother. Abuela is quite old, her powdered face peppered with large, brown sun spots and a lacework of fine lines like a spider's web, and she has tiny, barely perceptible, white hairs on her upper lip and chin. She's Señor Gómez's mother and she's come to stay so she can supervise the little English girl who is a guest in her son's home.

That's fine by me. She can supervise Crazy Concha too. I think she's on my side not hers because, when she finally stops raining kisses on me, she shouts at Concha and slaps her on the arm, hard, and then strokes *my* arm, and my face as well. I think she's telling her off for coming home from school without me.

Concha is furious. I'm not sure if it's because she's getting it in the neck (or the arm!) from Abuela for abandoning me or because I managed to get home at all. Let's face it, this is the second time she's hoped that I wouldn't make it. Maybe she thinks I'll just give up looking and get a flight home instead. (Not a bad idea, now I come to think about it!)

Anyway, she storms off to her room, slamming the door shut just in case I should suddenly get some mistaken idea in my head that she might want me to join her. Heavy rock music blasts out and Abuela screams at her granddaughter to turn it down, but she's ignored so she bangs on her door but it's locked. She rattles the handle and screams some more and Concha yells back at her. Honestly, it's like World War Three breaking out: if Mum screamed at me like that, I'd call ChildLine.

But then, Concha decides to turn the music down after all and Abuela beams at me and strokes my face lovingly again as if nothing has happened. They are all totally bonkers, this family. Señor Gómez walks in from work and Abuela covers him with dry, whiskery kisses and disappears into the kitchen. Peace is restored.

On the whole, it's nice having Abuela on board. She cooks us a massive dinner which unfortunately takes ages, so I sit down and make small talk with Señor

Gómez while we're waiting, my stomach rumbling with hunger. He's nice: he seems genuinely interested in me, asking me loads of questions about home and Mum, but I wish he wouldn't smoke so much. In the kitchen, Abuela clashes pots and pans around energetically and every so often shrieks out something incomprehensible in Spanish. She seems very excitable but Señor Gómez ignores her on the whole.

It's ten o'clock before we all sit down at the table and I am almost fainting with hunger. My mother would have a fit, eating at this time of night, but it was worth waiting for. There are loads of different dishes laid out – it's like a feast – and bottles of wine too. Concha immediately pours herself a glass of red and, not surprisingly, her father tells her off. But then he picks up the bottle and pours me a glass as well and I realize he's complaining about her manners, not her drinking habit! I take a cautious sip; I've never had wine before.

It tastes strong, fruity and sour, like plums that have been left to stew for too long. I hold it in my mouth for a while before I swallow. As it hits the pit of my empty stomach, warmth floods through my body. I immediately find myself relaxing and I smile at Señor Gómez who takes this as an invitation to top up my glass. I didn't mean for him to do that! If one sip has that effect on me, I'll be fast asleep after a whole glass.

Fortunately for me, Abuela clucks her disapproval and picks up my glass, pours most of it into her own and tops up mine with water. Then she does the same to Concha's. Concha objects loudly but Abuela screeches back at her and wins hands down. Concha shuts up and glares at me as if it's all my fault.

I don't know if it's because I've waited so long and I'm starving but I'm not kidding, the meal is really delicious. I was dead worried about trying Spanish food but it's amazing. Señor Gómez encourages me to try everything, and I kind of think Abuela has gone to all this trouble especially for me so I must oblige and I sample something from each plate. Some food I recognize, like *tortilla* (omlette) and *patatas* (potatoes, and Abuela has fried them with onion and ham, yummy!) and something that looks like the dish Adam brought to school today. When I point to it and ask, '*tripas?*' Abuela practically cries with pleasure and piles it on to my plate. That'll teach me to show off! Concha smirks but then I remember I've tried it and it's not bad and I tuck in.

In fact, it's all yummy. There are dainty little flans filled with asparagus and prawns, and plates of toast covered with things like *chorizo*, (a kind of spicy sausage) and *pimientos* (roasted red peppers), goats cheese and earthy black olives. I ask the name of everything I try, and do my best to commit it to memory. Señor Gómez translates for me and I find I'm eating stuff I've never had before in my life, like squid and anchovies. I even find myself crunching up tiny whole fish: by the time I spot a little round eye staring up at me through the breadcrumbs and discover they've still got their heads and tails on, it's too late to worry about it, I've eaten nearly all of them.

I wash it all down with my watered-down wine and sit back at last in my chair, sighing with pleasure. I'm stuffed. Abuela smiles at me approvingly, strokes my cheek for the umpteenth time, then turns to Concha who's hardly eaten a thing. She barks at her and Concha snarls back at her grandmother, gets up and stalks back into her room again. Abuela and Señor Gómez don't turn a hair.

They must be used to it.

I'm trying to be polite but honestly, I can hardly keep my eyes open. Abuela starts miming sleep movements at me, putting her palms together and resting her face on her hands, and I nod gratefully. But when I make a move towards my bedroom she jumps up and says, 'NO, no, no, no, no!!!!!' with much shaking of her head and takes my hand and leads me over to Concha's door and my heart plummets. I'd forgotten Abuela has taken over my bedroom.

To my surprise the door opens when she turns the handle. To my even bigger surprise, Concha is already tucked up in bed and fast asleep. The room is spick and span: the clothes have all been put away, the books and papers have been placed in a neat pile on the desk, the mugs and plates have disappeared. Opposite Concha's, a new bed has appeared, separated from hers by a chest of drawers. My pyjamas are neatly folded on top of its snowy white pillows and the room is bathed in a pool of soft, welcoming light from the bedside lamp on the chest of drawers. Abuela has been busy.

'Here!' she says briskly and opens the wardrobe door to show my clothes hanging neatly from the rail next to Concha's.

'Here!' she repeats and pulls open the top drawer of the chest to show me the rest of my stuff.

'Here!' She thrusts open a door in the corner to reveal an en-suite bathroom with fluffy white towels, just waiting to be used.

'*Gracias,*' I say gratefully and she kisses me again. I don't think I've ever been kissed so much in one day. I disappear into the bathroom, taking my pyjamas with me. When I come back, dressed for bed, she's still there, fussing. She moves around the room as I get into bed, adjusting the blind, collecting the clothes I've taken off (and I'm too tired to care whether she washes them or not), straightening the sheets on my bed.

Then she moves over to Concha and gazes down at her and her eyes soften. I lie there and watch as she strokes her granddaughter's brow tenderly, smoothing her hair away from her eyes, and utters gentle words under her breath, like a prayer. Then she kisses her gnarled fingers, presses them to the foot of the cross above Concha's bed and turns off the lamp.

I can feel a lump in my throat as she goes out of the bedroom, closing the door behind her.

Somebody loves Concha after all.

Maybe she's not that bad when you get to know her.

I sigh and settle down in the soft, comfy bed to sleep. It's been quite a day.

Next to me I hear a rustle of sheets.

'Has she gone?'

'What?'

'Silly old goat. Has she gone at last?'

As my eyes adjust to the darkness I dimly see Concha moving across the room towards me.

'What are you doing?'

She climbs up on to my bed, stepping on me in the process.

'Ouch!'

'Sshh! Idiot!'

She stretches to pull up the blind then opens the window. Moonlight floods into the room and I can see she is fully dressed. I prop myself up on my elbows to watch as she puts one foot out on the window ledge.

'Where are you going?'

'Mind your own business!' she says. 'Just keep your mouth shut!'

My eyes widen as she shuffles to the corner of the balcony and squats down as if she's going to jump. She can't, it's not possible, it's the third floor! The next second, I can't believe it, she launches herself into black space! There's a clunking sound. I lean out of the window, terrified of what I am about to see.

A few feet below, Concha's face grins up at me. She's hanging by her arms on the fire escape that comes down from the roof and as I watch she hauls herself safely through the railings and on to the iron steps. Then she's off, running sure-footedly down the steps to the street below.

A few seconds later, I hear an engine pop, pop, popping, then the sound of a scooter accelerating into the night.

Later on that night I wake suddenly from a troubled sleep in which I'm trying to find my way home (proper home I mean, to Mum) but the streets have turned their backs on me and I don't know where I am. I lie there for a moment, getting my bearings, and then I hear the door click shut and someone padding softly across the room towards me. First I freeze, then I scream. Very loudly. Well, you would, wouldn't you if you found some nutcase creeping round your bedroom in the dark? Wrong move. The intruder curses and lunges towards me, pressing down on my mouth with one hand and reaching for my neck with the other. He's trying to strangle me! In blind panic I shake my head from side to side and manage to free my mouth momentarily, long enough to bite down hard on the palm that's covering it. He lets go immediately, swearing at me in English.

In English!

Too late I realize who it is as Concha dives into her bed and pulls the sheet up tight round her neck. A split second later the light snaps on to reveal a fierce-looking Abuela, long white nightdress buttoned up to her throat, grey hair hanging round her shoulders, brandishing a plaster statue of a saint above her head. She's one scary sight I can tell you: I don't think she's planning to invite the prowler to kneel down and pray with her, that's for sure.

Behind her Señor Gómez appears in his boxer shorts.

'Girls? What's going on?'

'I'm sorry, I had a nightmare,' I gulp. Abuela crosses herself, raises her eyes to heaven and utters a pious prayer of thanks. Then she thrusts the statue into my hands and starts pulling the sheets straight on my bed, clucking all the time like a mother hen. Actually, it's quite nice and reassuring. I feel myself calming down, though I don't know what to do with the statue and I'm a bit scared she'll start stroking my face again and kissing me.

'It must have been a bad one. You screamed loud enough to wake the dead.' Señor Gómez's eyes shift to his daughter lying blissfully asleep in the bed next to mine and they narrow with suspicion. 'Concha?' he asks and she stirs and opens her eyes.

'Yes, Papa?' she says and smiles at him beatifically.

Wrong move. Concha is never that pleasant to anyone.

The next minute he strides over and sweeps the sheets off her bed to reveal Concha, fully-dressed. A verbal onslaught follows second to none I've yet witnessed but this time Concha is no match for the tongue-lashing she receives from her father, all in Spanish of course. Abuela screams at her too, waving her arms about alarmingly, and Concha bursts into tears. Her grandmother falls down on her knees, snatches the statue back out of my hands and implores it loudly, then starts wailing as well, only stopping occasionally to wipe her eyes and nose on my lacy bedspread.

I think this could have gone on all night but suddenly Abuela looks up through her tears and gasps with horror as it dawns on her that Señor Gómez is in the bedroom of the little *inglesa* dressed only in boxer shorts. She springs to her feet, very nimbly, I think, for someone her age, whips the now rather damp bedspread off my bed, wraps it around the waist of her errant son and shuffles him out of the room, repeating, '*Perdona, perdona, perdona* . . .' to me as they go.

Which leaves me alone with Concha. She turns her back on me: her shoulders are shaking and she's sniffing a lot. I stare at her glumly.

'I'm sorry.'

She ignores me.

'I didn't mean to get you into trouble.'

She turns over to scowl at me, her eyes swollen and red. 'You should have thought of that before you started wailing like a banshee.'

'You frightened me! How was I to know it was you creeping round my room?'

'Excuse me? *My* room? And anyway, who the hell did you think it was? You saw me go out, didn't you?'

'Yes, but I didn't see you come in! You went out through the window!' She sniffs scornfully. 'How did you get back?' I can't resist asking.

'Duh! Through the front door, idiot! I've got a key.'

Of course. She was hardly going to swing herself off the fire escape and back up through the window, was she? She's obviously done this before.

'Where did you go?'

'Out.' There's silence, then she says with a small smug smile, 'With my mates from school if you must know.'

Mates? Concha? I must've looked surprised because she adds crossly, 'Not the stupid little kids from my year. The older ones.'

'Who?'

'Pablo, Eduardo and some other guys.' She can't resist showing off. 'They race around on their scooters. We have a laugh. And now you've ruined it. My dad will be watching me like a hawk from now on!'

Maybe he should! No wonder Señor Gómez was

worried. Scooters can be dangerous, we'd been warned about those before we came out here. Plus anyone could see she was asking for trouble riding around at the dead of night with a gang of boys.

'Are you going out with Pablo?'

'Not yet.' Her face falls, then she rallies. 'It's only a matter of time though.'

She sounds confident but I'm not so sure. Going by what I saw of him yesterday, Pablo didn't give me the impression he was that interested in her. I turn over and wriggle down in my bed, trying to get comfortable again.

She probably will go out with him in the end though. I should think Concha always gets what she wants.

In the morning when I wake up I remember there is no school. It is Good Friday. That means I'm stuck with Concha all day on my own. But then I recall Fern and Dolores saying they were going to the beach today. In fact, everyone on exchange seemed to be planning to head for the beach with their host families. I cheer up. I expect we'd go too and I'd see them there.

At home Good Friday is often the first day of the school Easter holidays and I think of it as the start of spring. Mum has the day off work and we usually go shopping for new season clothes. We make a day of it, dressing up and catching the train to our nearest city shopping centre, having a nice lunch, sometimes getting our hair cut as well. It's a fun day out, one I look forward to after the dark days of winter, and for a second I feel a real pang and wish I was home with Mum. But then I pull the blind back to peer at the blue sky outside and remember my new bikini in the drawer beside my bed and I stretch luxuriously. I'm going to get a suntan today!

Cautiously I turn over to look at Concha, but she's still fast asleep, thank goodness, so I slip out of bed and go and have a shower in the en-suite bathroom. It's the same as the one in Abuela's room, the only difference being it's a bit more messy, the shelves overflowing with Concha's stuff. I turn on the shower and blast myself with hot water, then, I can't resist it, I investigate Concha's cache and help myself to a particularly gorgeous-smelling shower gel. Honey and olive: at least, I think that's the picture on the front. I debate washing my hair but decide it can last another day, especially if I'm going to the beach. Soon I've dried myself off in a lovely fluffy towel, scrubbed my teeth, moisturized myself with body cream with the same exquisite scent as the shower gel, got myself dressed and still, Concha hasn't stirred.

Unbelievably, after the feast last night, I'm starving. I've noticed that before, it's weird, the more you eat, the more you want to. And vice versa. The smell of coffee wafts into the bedroom, stirring my taste buds, so I go in search of breakfast, actually finding myself looking forward to those funny little cake things.

In the kitchen, Señor Gómez and Abuela are sitting at the table. Both of them look up and smile and say '*Buenos días*' and Abuela leaps up to find a bowl to fill with coffee for me. I sip it warily. If possible, it's even more bitter than yesterday's. I look around for the little cakes but there's no sign of them this morning. Abuela holds up her palms and shakes her head, saying something that sounds like '*el-b-air-ness-san-toe*', and I smile at her and nod and wonder what she means. I sip my coffee again and can't help wincing. Señor Gómez notices and stands up and reaches for something in the cupboard. Hurrah, I think, he's going to get me something to eat, but instead he hands me a packet of sugar lumps and I drop two glumly into my coffee and stir it with a spoon.

Is this all I'm going to get for my breakfast?

Maybe they're mad at me about last night. It wasn't my fault.

I sit there sipping my strong, though now very sweet coffee. Señor Gómez is reading the paper and Abuela appears to be praying, passing a string of rosary beads through her fingers and muttering repeatedly to herself in a fast, monotonous incantation. It's quite hypnotic actually, that is till the bedroom door crashes opens and

Concha emerges from her hideout.

She comes into the kitchen in her pyjamas, hair wild and unkempt, face dark and brooding. '*Buenos dias,*' chorus Señor Gómez and Abuela in unison but she ignores them and gets a bowl out of the cupboard. Then she opens another door and takes out a packet of cornflakes. So they do have normal food for breakfast! I feel myself perking up.

'NO! NO! NO! NO! NO! NO! NO!' shouts Abuela when she sees what she's doing, making me almost jump out of my skin. Even Concha looks startled.

'*¿Que?*' she barks.

'*¡El-b-air-ness-san-toe!*' Abuela repeats, or words to that effect.

Concha's eyebrows draw even closer together, so she looks like someone has painted a heavy black line across her brow. She places her hands on her hips and glares at her grandmother, 'SO?'

Her father yells back at her. Flip, they must be really angry with her if they're not going to let her eat anything today! But what about me? I didn't do anything wrong. Concha's not going to give in, she's made of sterner stuff than that. '*¿El Viernes Santo?*' she spits out, which I recognize is what Abuela has been saying but I'm still none the wiser. Then she turns to her father and says in English, 'So what if it is Good Friday?

70

We don't go to church anyway!'

Her father darts a quick look at Abuela. 'While my mother is here you will observe the fast and attend church!'

'Hypocrite!' yells Concha and hurls the cereal packet on to the floor in a temper.

I get it. Good Friday is a holiday in Spain but it is also, I remember now, quite literally, a holy day. That's where the word holiday comes from. Miss Martínez reminded us all before we left England that Easter is a very important festival time in Mediterranean countries. Good Friday commemorates the day that Christ died on the cross for us. Most people may have forgotten that in the UK, she said, but in Spain, a Catholic country, it has more significance.

'Some families may go to the beach,' she'd said. 'But others mark the day with fasting and abstinence.'

Trust me to be staying with one that fasts and abstains. Though I suspect it's Abuela who does this and the others have to follow suit. Abstains from what, I wonder? Whatever it is, it looks like I won't be getting a suntan after all.

As Concha stamps back into her bedroom, slams the door shut and turns the key, and Señor Gómez hammers on it in vain, I take her abandoned bowl and scoop up the spilt cornflakes off the floor. Then I go quietly into the lounge, closing the door behind me, and leave them to their latest argument.

It's surprising, I must be getting used to the bust-ups in this household already, they don't really seem to bother me any more. It's becoming like background music in a shop or public place – not of your taste, but you don't really notice it.

Or maybe today I have other priorities. While three generations of Gómezes hurl insults at each other, AGAIN, I'm more interested in eating up the discarded cornflakes. After all, I might not get fed again for the rest of the day.

It's all feast or famine here.

Actually we do get fed at lunchtime. I spend the morning watching children's television, which is not only entertaining but brilliant for improving my Spanish because the words are simple and they're pronounced really clearly. Then about midday, Abuela summons me to lunch. The others are already at the table, looking perfectly normal and harmonious. I can't believe the way they switch their emotions on and off in this family. I'm telling you, if I'd had a row with my mum like Concha had with her dad, I'd leave home for good.

Señor Gómez offers me what looks like a plate of doughnuts and even though I'm hungry, I hesitate. Cakes for breakfast, doughnuts for lunch, I'm going to go home looking like a Teletubby. Then survival instinct kicks in and I think, who cares so long as they feed me, and I take one anyway. When I take a bite, I have a surprise. It tastes of fish and it's delicious. There are ten on the plate.

Abuela has two, Señor Gómez has two, I have two out of politeness and Concha has four, greedy pig. I wish there were more. For afters we have little individual rice puddings. I hate rice pudding at home but I'm still hungry so I help myself and they turn out to be scrumptious, light and creamy and drizzled with honey.

Afterwards Señor Gómez looks at his watch. 'Time to get ready for the procession,' he says.

'A procession!' My face lights up. I remember now there was some kind of Easter festival on the itinerary. This sounds like fun. Maybe there will be floats and music and dancing in the streets and fireworks? Better than going to the beach, you could go there any day.

In Concha's bedroom I dither in front of the wardrobe.

'What do I wear?' I ask.

She looks at me blankly.

'I mean, it's a festival, isn't it? Something bright and colourful?'

'Yes,' she says, and a small smile plays on her face. 'Absolutely. The brightest and most colourful you can find.'

She disappears into the bathroom and I pull my stuff out of the wardrobe and examine it. I hate drawing attention to myself so I tend to wear dark or pastel colours. When Concha comes back, I'm still staring glumly at my clothes which are now strewn all over the bed.

'What's wrong?'

'I've got nothing to wear.'

'Think rich and vibrant,' she says and scans my clothes. 'Ah, I see what you mean. Not to worry.' She throws her wardrobe doors open. 'Borrow something of mine.'

'Are you sure?' I'm surprised by her generosity.

'Of course. Try this.' She pulls out a scarlet, halter-neck, polka-dot top, the sort of thing I would never wear in a month of Sundays at home, then she chucks a pair of bright yellow micro shorts at me. 'Put these on with them.'

She must be joking. Doubtfully, I do as she says. To my surprise she jumps up and down with excitement.

'You look amazing!' she squeals. 'Your legs go on for ever, it's not fair!' For a second she looks envious then the next minute she's dug out some jewelled flip-flops, a stripey bag and a pair of oversized shades for me. I stare at myself in the mirror, full of anxiety.

'It's not too much, is it? I don't look tarty?'

'Not at all,' she says, attaching huge hooped earrings to my lobes. 'You look spectacular!'

I'm still not sure, but she's so pleased I haven't the heart to refuse. Anyway, today is different. I am in Spain, I am going to a festival and nobody knows me! Time to be daring.

'Thanks, Concha!' I say and decide that she's not so bad after all.

'All yours,' she says, indicating the bathroom, and pulls off her top. 'I'd better get ready myself. Take your time!'

By the time I've cleaned my teeth and put on some lippy and eye make-up and sprayed myself with Concha's perfume (I've got to stop doing this, it must be the Tira in me!), she's ready and is waiting for me in the hall with the others.

When I come out of the bedroom I stop dead. So do they. They stop talking too, in Abuela's and Señor Gómez's case because their jaws have dropped by a metre. They look like three crows, all dressed in black, with their beaks wide open, only the cawing has stopped.

Señor Gómez is dressed in a dark, sober suit and a black tie, as if he's going to a funeral.

Abuela is wearing a black dress, a grey shawl and a curiously high comb in her hair, like a headdress.

Concha has brushed her hair neatly to one side and is wearing a dark skirt that reaches to below her knees, a black cardigan that covers her arms, sensible shoes and she is looking completely un-Concha-like except for the big wide, sneery grin that is taking over her face.

Abuela's eyes round with horror and she starts yapping

at me like an excitable dog. Señor Gómez mutters something out of the side of his mouth to Concha who wipes the smile off her face before he can see it and starts muttering words of concern, in Spanish of course, back to him. And I stand there like a lemon.

From the waist down, that is. From the waist up I'm more like Minnie Mouse.

Ever been had?

'I'll go and change!' I splutter and make to dive back into the bedroom. But Señor Gómez looks at his watch, gasps and shouts, 'No! No time!' and hustles us all straight out of the door, in my case not too gently I notice, as his hand propels me forward in what seems very much like a shove to me. In the lift Abuela glares at me and protests to Señor Gómez who tries to avoid looking in my direction. As we emerge into the sunlight outside, some workmen whistle at me and he practically bundles me into the back of the car as my cheeks flare with embarrassment.

Next to me Concha smirks. 'You've gone red,' she says. Then she adds, 'By the way, stop helping yourself to my perfume.'

My cheeks go redder still. Between us, Abuela gets her beads out again, closes her eyes and starts to pray.

I get the distinct impression that she is praying for me.

* * *

We park a little way out of town and join a big queue of people outside a huge, old church. I feel so conspicuous. Everyone, and I mean everyone, is dressed in black. Most of the women are wearing high headdresses like Abuela and some of them have veils covering their hair as well. The men are all in dark suits and the children are in dark clothes too, except for the babies. They look at me like I'm from another planet. The kids nudge each other and laugh but some of the adults, the old women especially, mutter crossly when they see me in my brightly-coloured shorts and halter-neck, my back, legs and shoulders on display.

I turn to Concha, furious. 'Liar! Why didn't you tell me we were going to a funeral!'

'Don't call me a liar!' she says, looking just as angry. 'It's not a funeral, stupid, it's a procession, just like my father said. It is Good Friday, after all. It's not my fault you decided to dress like you were going to a rave!'

'I thought it was a festival!'

'You shouldn't jump to conclusions then, should you?'

'You made me dress like this! You said I looked sensational!'

'No I didn't. I said you looked spectacular. And you do,' she points out helpfully. 'You look as if you're making a spectacle of yourself!'

Trust me to get as my exchange partner the one

Spanish kid who speaks English better than I do!

This is really, truly, all my worst nightmares rolled into one. I am totally the centre of unwanted attention in the middle of this crowd of people, some of whom are merely curious, others who are clearly offended by the amount of my flesh on display on this, the most sombre day of the Christian calendar. I am torn between wishing I could curl up and die and wanting to punch the lights out of Concha's smug-looking face.

Which is not a good idea, because she'd hit me back. And a catfight between an English girl and a Spanish girl is probably not what Good Friday, or the exchange programme for that matter, is all about. So instead I try to hide myself in the middle of a sea of sober black clothes, though a startling red skimpy top with white polka dots and bright yellow shorts are not really the best camouflage.

At least when Pablo and Eduardo walk past, I have the satisfaction of seeing the annoyance in Concha's eyes as they spot me immediately in the crowd (I wonder why?) and show their appreciation of my outfit by whistling and catcalling at me. 'Come to the beach with us, beautiful *Inglesa*!' Pablo shouts and Concha glowers. Abuela does too, then suddenly, in a fit of inspiration, she whips her shawl from her shoulders and wraps it around me.

I don't mind. It covers me completely and I grip it tight so no one can see what I'm wearing underneath. After that I manage to drop back a bit in the parade and then nobody takes any notice of me and I just become part of the crowd.

And here's the thing. This procession, though it's completely different from what I expected – no dancing, no floats, no fireworks or razzmataz – well, actually, it blows my mind.

I suppose I could've worked it out really. I mean, I know what Easter's all about, I'm not that ignorant. On Easter Sunday, Christ rose from the dead but before that, on Good Friday, he died on the cross. It occurs to me it wasn't actually that good a Friday for him.

Anyway, I, like millions of others at home, might normally spend the day going shopping and looking forward to stuffing myself on overpriced chocolate in two days' time, but out here loads of people really go to town keeping alive the real meaning of Easter. They even get someone to pretend to be Christ and carry the cross himself. That's what the procession is for. As I watch, a guy dressed in a loin cloth, with long hair and a beard, comes out of the church and takes up position at the front of the procession. Lots of people in the queue genuflect or bow their heads as he passes. Four men carry a huge, wooden cross out of the church behind him and lever it on to his shoulders.

'It's a great honour to be chosen,' whispers Señor Gómez when he sees my startled face. He's talking to me again now I've stopped flaunting my body and am modestly covered. I feel so sorry for this guy, the cross is massive, it's like carrying two big trees by yourself, and he staggers under its weight. Then, when he's got it balanced, he lurches forward, half carrying, half dragging the cross behind him, his body bowed over with the weight of it all. A band starts up and the whole crowd moves after him in a huge swell of mournful sound.

It's boiling hot now and I'm starting to swelter under the shawl. I don't know how the man carrying the cross can stand it. Sweat is already trickling down my face; what must it be like for him? My respect grows as we follow him slowly through the cobbled streets under the blazing sun. I try to find cool pockets of shade to step into as we move, but he can't do that as he trudges resolutely on, bearing his heavy load. All along the route we are watched with curiosity by rows of spectators, some of them respectful locals, others obvious tourists sporting metres of exposed flesh.

'What a weirdo!' sneers an English voice. A blond, overweight kid, flushed with the heat, passes comment to his bored-looking sister, as he takes a gigantic mouthful of ice cream and gazes uncomprehendingly after the man bearing the cross. She sniggers back at him obligingly and swigs her can of Coke. I feel a surge of rage. How dare they? Don't they get what's going on here? Have some respect!

As we pass them, I feel an elbow in my ribs and I'm knocked off balance, my foot coming down hard on to the girl's toe. She squeals with pain and lifts her leg, grabbing her brother to steady herself, and his ice cream falls, upended, on to the ground. He shouts out at her in anger. Beside me Concha giggles and when I turn to look at her, she flashes me a wide, complicit grin.

I try not to, I mean that's not exactly what all this is about, is it? Plus I'm still mad at her for making me look like a freak. But, it's no good, I can't resist grinning back.

The thing is, I'm no mere onlooker, me. Not like they are, with their Cokes and ice creams and scornful words. They may stare bemused at us as we pass, then move away to seek out the next item of holiday entertainment, but me, I'm part of this. I may be suffocating under the shawl but I daren't loosen it, I *won't* loosen it, because I'm part of this procession, part of this *thing* that is going on here that I don't really understand, but can tell is something special by the weeping of Abuela and the other women around me and the deep, desolate sound of hundreds of men's voices, singing in unison.

We move on slowly through the town in the searing

heat of the afternoon and I lose all sense of time. At last, we find ourselves back at the church again. Part of me is relieved. I was starting to get worried that the poor guy was actually going to be crucified on some Spanish hill before my very eyes. But part of me is disappointed that we, at the tail of the procession, can't get into the packed church for the rest of the ceremony, me who can count on one hand how many times I've been in a church in my life.

Abuela is tired now after all that walking, clinging to her son's arm for support like a wilting bloom. Señor Gómez pats her hand. 'Time to go home, I think,' he says to me and turns around to look for Concha.

She is nowhere to be seen.

Concha's really done it this time. Señor Gómez is furious with her. And *she* is furious with me.

Well, I had to say something, didn't I? Poor Abuela was absolutely knackered after she'd walked literally miles round those streets in the blazing sun following that cross. She looked as if she was going to collapse any second, but she wouldn't go home till we'd found Concha. She wanted to trail around town again looking for her, convinced she'd got lost or been kidnapped or something. Nobody seemed to have a clue where she'd got to. To me it was obvious.

In the end, I say quietly, 'Maybe she's gone to the beach?'

Señor Gómez looks at me as if I'm from another planet.

'The beach?' he repeats.

'Yes. You know . . . I just thought . . . Pablo and Eduardo . . . the boys . . .'

Señor Gómez lets out a stream of curses. Now I know who Concha gets it from. He pushes Abuela and me into the back of the car and sets off at high speed. The car swings us from side to side and, beside me, Abuela lurches about all over the place, like a loose ball in a game of bagatelle. I move closer to her and slip my arm through hers in order to keep her steady. She clutches me gratefully. It's probably just as well if we get her home quickly.

Only we're not going home. To my alarm I suddenly realize we are making a detour to the beach. Señor Gómez seems to know where he's going. We stop at the promenade, next to a big flagpole, and he opens the back door and tells me to get out. Then he walks me to the railings and we stop as he scours the beach in front of him. I spot them immediately, standing out amongst the families on the sand, a big crowd of raucous kids from school, dressed in bikinis and board shorts, flirting, laughing, mucking about together on a gloriously sunny day.

Concha is there in a red bikini, chatting to Pablo and Eduardo of course. I can see Fern and Dolores too with Holly, Adam, Nacho, Jason and the others. Fern sees me and jumps up and down, waving and shrieking, 'Jaime! Jaime! Over here!' Concha looks up when she hears my name and her face changes from surprise to anger when she spots her father beside me. Señor Gómez roars her name and everyone stares. Concha swears audibly then picks up her discarded clothes from the sand and flounces towards us. The kids laugh and cheer.

I'm kind of surprised that she comes so compliantly but when I see Señor Gómez grab her elbow as soon as she appears on the promenade and frogmarch her to the car, I understand why. He's done this before.

He thrusts her into the front seat and straps her into her seat belt like he's tying her up so she can't get away. By now she is sobbing with rage and frustration. Abuela passes her a tiny lace handkerchief but she throws it on the floor of the car and wipes her face instead on her bundle of clothes. Señor Gómez grabs her cardigan and shoves it over her, telling her (I think) to cover up, in a stream of angry Spanish.

By the time we get home, things have quietened down a bit. Concha defiant, her eyes nearly as red as her bikini, marches straight to her room and locks the door. Señor Gómez hammers on it for a while, then gives up and goes into the lounge and switches on the television. The sound of a football match commentary fills the flat. Abuela goes off to lie down.

I am left, once more, on my own.

I sit in the kitchen. There is nowhere else to go and there is nothing else to do. The clock ticks on and on and

I stare blankly at the white walls and the blue mosaic tiles and think I am going to go mad.

My tummy rumbles. At home it would be teatime now. All I've had to eat today is two cod buns and a small pot of rice pudding. I'm starving.

I stand up and look inside the cupboards. They are full of jars with weird things inside them – pickled vegetables and bottled fruit mainly. I open the fridge and it's packed with stuff, but it's mostly raw meat and fish, garlic, peppers, onions, courgettes, aubergines and loads of other things I don't recognize. Plenty of ingredients for meals, but nothing I can nibble at. No bread, no crisps, no biscuits. What am I supposed to do?

I pull my mobile out of my pocket, deciding that I'm going to call Fern, Mum, Miss Martínez, anyone! Though I know it will cost me the earth. But even that option isn't open to me. My battery's dead and I realize too late, I've forgotten to pack my charger.

My throat hurts like it does when I'm trying not to cry. Despite my best intentions, I can feel my eyes welling up, then two fat tears spill over and run down my cheeks.

I want my mum!

Easter weekend passes in a bit of a blur. Surprisingly after the heat wave on Friday, it's lashing it down on Saturday and we spend the day indoors, except for Señor Gómez who I guess goes out to work. He's certainly not around.

In the morning I mooch around the flat, going stir crazy, then after lunch, when Abuela has had her siesta, I end up baking with her, for something to do. Concha refuses to get up till the afternoon then, when she sees what we're doing, she looks disdainful and makes some cutting remark which is wasted on me because it's in Spanish, while she helps herself to a bowl of cereal. Abuela shouts in protest, but Concha ignores her and the old lady mumbles away to herself then forgets all about her wayward granddaughter as she shows me how to prepare exquisite little sweet pastries and the small portions of tasty savouries known as *tapas*. It's fun.

That evening we eat them up, the three of us, while we watch DVDs in Spanish – a couple of rom coms, Concha's choice of course. I'm surprised to discover I can more or less follow them if I concentrate hard. Mind you, it's not easy concentrating, sitting next to Abuela. Her reaction to the films is hilarious. She really lives and breathes them, never taking her eyes off the screen for a second, sucking in her breath and clucking with disapproval at the more explicit content and laughing out loud at the funny bits, a comical, high-pitched half-peal, half-cackle, that makes you laugh too. Even Concha glances at her with amusement. She still hasn't spoken to me since she was dragged off the beach the previous day but to be honest, I'm past caring. I'm enjoying hanging out with Abuela. I wish I had a granny like her.

I wish I had a granny full stop!

The food is delicious. I notice that Concha is more than happy to gobble it up even though she looked down her nose at us making it. Midway through the second film I can sense that Abuela is starting to nod off on the sofa beside me. It's tiring work, watching DVDs! When Señor Gómez comes home at last, looking mellow and happy and smelling of wine, he finishes off what's left of the food with a glass of brandy, and compliments Abuela on her culinary skills.

'No, no, no!' she protests and flaps her hands at me.

'You did it?' he asks in surprise. 'I am impressed!' I smile at him happily and snuggle back down next to Abuela on the couch, not wanting to miss the film. Abuela's hand reaches out drowsily to pat my knee then soon she gives a little snore and falls asleep again.

That night, when we are tucked up in bed, Concha's voice breaks the silence. 'My grandmother likes you,' she says, in the darkness.

'I like her too,' I answer.

Everything is still.

'My father likes you as well,' she continues. Her voice sounds hollow.

'Thanks.' I can feel my heart beating hard. Concha has

never been this forthcoming before. After a while I ask, tentatively, 'Why are you called Gómez López?'

'We take our mother's surname too. My father's surname is Gómez . . .'

'. . . and your mother's surname is López?'

'Yes.'

'What's her first name?'

'Mercedes.'

'Like the car?'

'Yes.' She chuckles. 'Just like the car. My mother is beautiful and graceful and very high-powered.'

I made her laugh! Carried away, I reply, 'How much does she do to the litre?' Then I immediately wish I could take the words back. What a stupid thing to say! But it's OK, Concha sees the funny side.

'Not very much. She is too high-maintenance.'

I lift my head and strain to see her in the darkness. 'Concha? Why don't you live with her any more?'

Silence. Then a retort, as sharp and shocking as the blade of a knife, slicing through the delicate tissue of communication that was growing between us.

'Mind your own business. Creep!'

She makes a huge play of turning over and settling down in her bed, like I'm so beneath contempt, she can't even be bothered to stay awake to be rude to me any more.

But for all that, I don't think she does go to sleep. Because much later on she's still tossing and turning in her bed and keeping me awake.

The next day is Easter Sunday and we get up to go to Mass. We go back to the church we went to on Good Friday, only this time we actually get to go inside. It's big and old, with a vast, soaring ceiling and a great high altar decorated with vases of blue, white and yellow flowers. There are rows and rows of wooden pews, all polished to perfection, and around the sides of the church in the dim light stand life-size plaster statues of saints with tall, wrought-iron tiers of candles before them, waiting to be lit.

Above the altar I can see the cross, back in its rightful place now, and as I follow the Gómezes into a pew, I surprise myself by dipping my knee respectfully before it as they do. It seems the natural thing to do. Then I sit down and watch the sun filtering through the stained-glass windows, lighting up the dancing dust and casting shafts of sparkling colour on the heads of the people in front of me. It's beautiful.

The Mass starts and there's a lot of standing and singing and recitation of prayer as everyone joins in. In front of us I spot the guy who played Christ and am doubly relieved to see he hasn't been crucified after all, because he's got a wife and kids. Today he doesn't look quite so Christ-like: he's wearing a trendy shirt and blue jeans with his hair tied back in a ponytail, and he's holding a baby and hanging on to a little boy at the same time, trying to stop him running around. His wife looks pregnant again, though maybe she's just fat; she's really pretty anyway. They look so happy.

Loads of families are in church, all in their best clothes, most of them with babies in their arms. These Spanish parents smother them with kisses all the time and stroke them too, their hair, their clothes, their fat, brown legs, anything they can touch, like they can't get enough of them. I watch the Christ man as he tickles his baby and she gurgles back at him and tugs at his hair, her eyes full of love. I glance sideways at Concha. Did anyone ever play with her like that? She feels me looking at her and scowls.

Afterwards we join up with another family and go for lunch in a restaurant. The Spanish take their feast days literally. The food is delicious but I feel a bit awkward. The other family speak only Spanish. Señor Gómez tries to include me in the conversation but it's difficult, they speak so fast. I think they are all excited at being together because soon they are all rabbiting away nineteen to the dozen, even Concha, and they forget about me. I feel out of it. I feel alone.

That evening, back at the flat, I'm at a loose end. Señor Gómez is doing some work on his laptop, Abuela's dozing in the chair, Concha's in her room as usual. Should I watch telly? Is it OK to switch it on? It's so weird being a guest in someone else's house, you feel you're being cheeky doing the normal things you'd do at home. I let out a heavy sigh as I sit in the lounge. I don't even want to watch it, I don't understand it anyway. I know what I really want to do.

I want to go into my bedroom and write to Mum, but I don't like to because Concha's there.

Out in the hall, the phone rings. Abuela jumps up and answers it. 'Jaime?' she says, puzzled, then screeches, 'Jaime! Jaime! Mama! Mama! Mama!' at the top of her voice like the house is on fire. I bound out of my chair and grab the phone from her.

'Mum!'

'Jaime!'

It's fabulous hearing her voice. I can't believe she's thousands of miles away. 'You sound like you're in the next room!' I say in delight.

'So do you! Are you having a good time? What have you been up to?'

I tell her in great detail all about school and the flat and the procession and going out for lunch and baking with Abuela. We natter on for ages.

'Well, it sounds as if they're looking after you!' says Mum finally. 'By the way, what's Concepción Inmaculada like?'

'Who?'

'Your exchange partner!' laughs Mum.

'Oh, Concha!' Opposite me the bedroom door opens and Concha's head pokes out. 'What?' she asks crossly, hearing her name.

'Nothing!' I say and point at the phone in my hand. She glares at me and slams the door shut. I poke my tongue out at the closed door.

'Jaime?' says Mum's voice anxiously at the end of the phone.

'Nice,' I say wildly. What else could I say? 'She's nice.'

'Oh that's good,' she says with relief. 'Because you never know, do you?'

Huh! That's not what she'd told me. 'A nice little Spanish girl,' she'd said, that's what I'd get.

'What have you been doing then?' I ask, changing the subject, though I know the answer already. Missing me!

'Oh you know, nothing much.' She sounds vague. 'I went to the cinema on Thursday. And I was out for dinner last night.'

'You gadabout!' Mum never goes anywhere, except for work.

She laughs. 'Well, the place is so quiet without you. I've

got to do something!' See? I knew she was missing me!

'Who did you go with?'

In the background I hear the doorbell ring. Mum says, all a fluster, 'Oh there's the door, Jaime. I'd better go, darling, I didn't realize the time. We've been on the phone for ages! I'll phone you again soon. Glad to hear you're having such a good time. Love you!'

The phone goes dead. I stare blankly at it then replace it carefully in its holder. That was a bit sudden, wasn't it? And who was that at the door? It sounded like she was off out again to me. She never goes out! Where was she off to at this time of night?

And, more important still, who was she going out with?

Once Easter weekend is over, the days gallop by. I guess in my head it was a bit of a milestone getting that weekend over and done with. Like hauling myself slowly over the hump of a hump-backed bridge. I'm on the downward slope now and I've speeded up. Only a week to go and I'll be home again.

Monday we spend on the beach with the others; apparently it's OK in the Gómez López household to take off and have fun with your mates at the beach on Easter Monday, just not on Good Friday. Now that Lent is well and truly over, we can do what we like. I reckon this is partly because poor old Abuela is finding it harder than she thought it would be looking after us all and partly because Señor Gómez has had enough of being cooped up in the flat with his mother and two emotionally volatile teenage girls. I mean, Concha's permanently a smouldering firework waiting to go off and even I had a bit of a cry when I came off the phone to Mum on Sunday night. Señor Gómez buried his head in the paper and pretended not to notice. Concha did though. She offered me a chocolate. I was so surprised I said no, and she looked embarrassed, then she looked cross, but I was too miserable to care.

But then the next day the exchange kids have a beach day and it's fun. Señor Gómez drops us off and says he will pick us up later. The teachers are on the beach already, supposedly to keep an eye on us, but they're in holiday mode and don't interfere too much. Miss Martínez looks stunning in an effortless way, wearing a tight-fitting T-shirt over her bikini, cool shades and her long dark hair scraped up into a high ponytail. Everyone is there, the boys with their eyes glued to Miss Martínez, hoping she will take her T-shirt off. Fern says she'd had a bit of a weep after her mum phoned on Easter Sunday too, even though she was having a ball at Dolores's house. Then Holly admits she's cried too because she spoke to her mum but not her dad and she wants them to stay together, and even Adam says he's missing Marmite, his dog and his Play Station, in that order.

Anyway, after discovering we're all homesick, we cheer up and have a brilliant time, sunbathing, splashing in the sea and messing about on the beach with the Spanish kids. Most of the girls, me included, get ambushed by the boys during the course of the day and are carried, kicking and screaming, down the beach to be dunked in the sea. They don't dare do it to Concha; she'd have flattened them if they tried. Here's the strange thing though: when I come back from my dunking, totally saturated, hair hanging in wet rats' tails round my shoulders, freezing cold and still spluttering, she looks, I don't know . . . envious?

Nah, I must have been imagining it.

We spend all day in the sun, fooling about and playing beach volleyball. To my delight I discover I'm good at that too. Concha won't join in, even though I ask her to. She's sulking for some reason. Then, in the early evening, just as we are getting hungry, the exchange families start drifting down to the beach laden with baskets of food and we all have a barbie, right there on the sand. It's awesome. There's stacks of food: burgers, hot dogs, steaks, kebabs, and sardines, plucked fresh out of buckets and skewered in rows over the fire on long sticks, all served with hunks of crusty bread.

'No veg, no salad. My kind of food!' says Adam, taking a huge bite of fish burger and smiling at us blissfully with a sardine tail sticking out of his mouth. I take a photo of him and then snap loads of us all with our arms round each other. There are two big bins full of ice too, with cans of Coke for us in one and bottles of beer for the adults in the other. Of course, the boys try to get the beer too, protesting they're allowed it at home, but the girls get their own back for the dunkings and shout them down. It's great meeting all the exchange families. Fern is so lucky, Dolores's mum is lovely, and Holly's partner, Ana, has got the cutest little sister. Then all of a sudden, I see Señor Gómez helping Abuela down the steps to the beach and I grab Fern.

'Look! Here's Abuela and Señor Gómez! Come and meet them!' I run over to the steps to introduce her. Señor Gómez does his little bow thing and shakes Fern's hand. He looks nice this evening, younger and more relaxed in T-shirt and shorts. Abuela pats Fern on the cheek, then takes my arm gratefully. I feel quite proud, escorting her carefully across the sand to meet the teachers. It's funny, I've never had anything to do with old people before, I think I'd be embarrassed at home to be seen with one hanging off my arm, but over here it's different. Concha doesn't think so though: she doesn't even bother to come over to her grandmother and say hello.

When I introduce them to Miss Martínez, Señor Gómez's eyes widen in appreciation. Honestly, he's so obvious, he's as bad as the boys, only they've got an excuse, they're full of hormones. Concha's father is about the same age as my mother, he should be over all that. He opens a beer and starts chatting away to her in Spanish, forgetting all about poor old Abuela, so I find a chair for her to sit down on nearby. After a while, she's joined by more grannies who've been brought to the beach with their families, and soon, they're coming down in droves.

'Miss Martínez? Are there more old people here than at home?' asks Fern pointedly, as an old woman joins the throng and kicks Fern's towel out of the way, planting her chair in the space and settling herself comfortably down in it. Miss Martínez laughs at Fern's indignant face.

'Looks like, doesn't it? No, the fact is that old people are an important and valued part of the family in Spain. They tend not to be shut away in old people's homes, like they are in the UK.'

'Shame!' says Concha loudly. She's standing behind me, earwigging the conversation. Miss Martínez glances at her in surprise and Señor Gómez looks annoyed.

'Concha!' he says. 'Will you behave?'

Miss Martínez moves away, embarrassed by the family confrontation, and Concha flings herself down on her towel, a smug grin on her face. It occurs to me she's got what she wanted again. A bit of attention.

Plus, she's managed to stop her dad chatting up Miss Martínez.

I watch her as she puts on her headphones and turns over on to her back, propping herself up on her elbows to listen to her iPod. Then Fern says, 'Coming for a last swim, Jaime? Everyone's going in.'

'Yeah! Wait for me!' I pull my top over my head and throw it down on the sand beside Concha. I hesitate for a second, wondering if I should ask her to join us, though nobody else has, but she ignores me, looking pointedly past me at the sea with a supercilious expression on her face. Most of the boys have already dived in and the girls are squealing and jumping up and down in the waves, 'Come on, Jaime!' yells Fern, then she and Dolores run back and grab me by the hands and the three of us race down the beach together, screaming at the tops of our voices, to fall with an enormous splash into the sea. It's heart-stoppingly cold but I'm laughing so much it doesn't matter a bit and at that moment I realize I'm loving this exchange holiday, I'm having so much fun and I'm so, so glad that I came!

We spend ages in the sea which now feels less like a freezer and more like a warm bath; the sun has actually set by the time we get out. Everything's been packed away and Dolores's family and the Gómezes are waiting to go. Concha's already in the car, still listening to music and looking fed up. I wrap myself in the towel Abuela is holding out for me and laugh as she gives me a rub, like I'm about six years old. Actually, it's nice to be looked after. I give Fern and Dolores damp, salty hugs and promise to see them the next day, waving to them as they drive away.

On the back seat of the car, I snuggle happily inside my towel, and Señor Gómez turns up the heater to keep me warm, whistling to himself tunelessly. Abuela, replete with evening sun and gossip, hums away contentedly to the song on the radio as we set off for home. It's been a lovely day.

Not everyone's enjoyed it though. Beside me, headphones still clamped firmly to her ears, Concha stares coldly out of the window.

The next day we're back at school. They just have the Easter weekend off here and take their holiday at the end of term in a couple of weeks' time. I don't mind, I love it in school. The days fly by. We play basketball every lunchtime and I get really good at it, becoming one of the top shooters. It does wonders for my confidence, hearing kids, both Spanish and English, cry, '¡TIRA! ¡TIRA! ¡TIRA!' every time I get my hands on the ball.

My growing self-assurance carries into other lessons too, especially Spanish. I'm definitely picking up the language quicker than anyone else. One day I get carried away though. The teacher asks the class in Spanish, 'Does anyone have any pets?' and no one answers because they don't understand the question. But I do, so

I shoot my hand up even though, in actual fact, I don't have one.

'Do you have any pets, Jaime?' the teacher repeats.

'*Sí*,' I answer proudly. '*Tengo un . . .*' I rack my brains to conjure a pet in Spanish out of my limited vocabulary. '. . . *Tengo un lápiz!*'

There is a stunned silence, then the Spanish kids start laughing. I look around perplexed. What have I said? Concha, needless to say, is shrieking the loudest.

'Are you sure you mean *lápiz*, Jaime?' the teacher asks. Even she's trying not to laugh, I can tell.

'Yeah. I think so,' I say bewildered. 'I have a pet rabbit *Tengo un lápiz . . .*' My voice trails away as everyone laughs again.

The teacher shakes her head, smiling. 'In French *lapin* is rabbit. But in Spanish, *lápiz* is pencil.'

I clap my hand to my mouth. Serves me right for showing off! I have just announced to the whole class that I have a pet pencil! Next to me Concha is still sniggering away. But, in front of me, Dolores and Ana turn around and smile kindly, and behind me, Sergio claps me on the shoulder. The lesson moves on.

And guess what? I didn't go red!

It's not all school, though I wouldn't mind if it was. They try to reschedule some of the trips because our disastrous coach journey has mucked up the itinerary, so we spend most of the time in school but occasionally we're whisked off on various outings. We go up into the mountains to see an authentic Spanish village which allegedly hasn't changed for centuries, though the Spanish kids tell us no one actually lives there, it's just a set-up for the tourists. Another day we visit an art gallery where we gaze in confusion at seriously weird paintings of people with giant eyes and lips.

'Call this art!' scoffs Jason. 'Little kids can do better than this at home!'

He's rewarded for his artistic critique by a dead arm from Sergio, his exchange partner, who doesn't take kindly to his national pride being dented.

The day before we're due to leave we're taken to the market to buy souvenirs. It's magic: apart from loads of stands piled high with food, especially fruit and veg, there are stalls selling jewellery, fans, castanets, Peruvian pan-pipes, shoes, leather bags, multicoloured pottery and bottles of aloe vera. We wander around, tasting the specialities, having our hair beaded and selecting our presents. It's hilarious: some of us have not really got the hang of this bargaining malarkey. Holly walks away happily clutching a necklace made of buttons oblivious to the fact that she's been bargaining UP instead of down! I find a stall selling embroidered tablecloths like the ones Abuela uses and take a long time choosing one, then negotiating the right price for it. I'm proud of myself when the stall owner finally folds it up and hands it to me and I count out my euros.

'Who's that for?' asks Concha, who's been hanging around behind me, bored out of her skull. To be honest, I wish she'd just stop trailing after me and get lost.

'My mum.'

'Tat!' she sneers and turns away to point out another stall. 'Now these,' she says, 'are much better quality.' Why didn't she tell me that before? Crossly, I stuff the tablecloth into my stripey bag and make a rude gesture behind her back. I am rewarded by some of the Spanish girls who spot me and start giggling. Concha glances up at me suspiciously and I smile blandly at her. Surprised, she gives me a fleeting half-smile in return. The Spanish girls giggle some more.

I feel mean then.

After a while we realize the boys are nowhere to be seen. Finally we catch up with them coming out of the livestock area, where they are selling chickens and ducks, rabbits, sheep and goats.

'Pooh! What are you doing here? It stinks,' remarks Fern, wrinkling up her nose.

'Nothing!' say Jason and Adam simultaneously.

We immediately stare at them in suspicion. 'What are you up to?' asks Holly.

'Nothing!' reiterates Jason but Adam, unable to resist showing off, puts his hand in his jeans pocket.

'Just doing some souvenir shopping!' he says and pulls out a yellow ball of fluff. He cups it in his hand and it rises up on tiny stilt-like legs, shakes itself out, opens a tiny beak and cheeps. We all stand around drooling over the tiny chick standing on his palm.

'Who's it for?' I ask, stroking its soft downy feathers with my finger.

'My sister.'

'Which one?'

'Jenna.'

'You've got two sisters. What about the other one?'

'Dah-dah!' He brings out a second chick from his other pocket with a flourish, like a magician pulling doves out of a hat. 'I got one for Jude too. Here, hold this.' He dumps it into my hands and rummages about in the pocket of his hoody. 'Look what I've got for my brother!' He pulls out a scaly gekko which flicks its tongue out and regards us balefully, with cold, beady eyes. Involuntarily, we take a step back.

'Yuk! Put it away! What are you giving your mum? A goat?'

'Nah,' says Adam, sliding the lizard back into his pocket. 'I've run out of money. She'll have to share.'

'What have you got?' The front of Jason's hoody is

starting to writhe alarmingly. Carefully, he extracts a duckling, grey and fluffy, much bigger than the tiny chicks. The duckling quacks at us in surprise.

'I could only afford the one,' he says regretfully. 'They're dead pricey these.'

'How do you think you're going to get them home?' asks Concha, scornfully. 'You won't get them through customs.'

The boys look at each other and shrug.

'We'll manage.'

'What's going on here?' says a voice. Jason stuffs the duckling back inside his hoody just as Mr Evans appears behind us, with Miss Martínez in tow. It quacks loudly in protest. Jason starts quacking too. I drop the chick I'm holding into my stripey bag and Adam, seeing what I've done, tips the other one in as well. Concha, who's standing next to me, sees it all.

'Why are you quacking, Jason?' asks Mr Evans, puzzled.

'He's nuts, Sir. Look what I've bought.' Holly thrusts her bag in front of him and starts pulling out necklaces and bracelets. 'And me!' chips in Fern and pushes a bottle of aloe vera under his nose. She twists the top. 'Smell that!' she instructs. Mr Evans looks a bit disconcerted but does as he's told. With his attention diverted, Adam and Jason seize the opportunity to sidle away. My carrier bag is cheeping so I go to follow them but Miss Martínez stops me.

'What have you bought, Jaime?' she asks kindly.

'Me, Miss? Nothing . . .' I say. 'Just a tablecloth for my mum.'

'Oh, I want to get a tablecloth. Let's have a look,' she says eagerly, reaching out a hand for my bag. Involuntarily, I put it behind my back.

'No,' I say wildly. 'It's a surprise!'

She stares at me astonished. I can feel my colour rising as everyone turns to look at me. Suddenly, Concha steps forward and takes her by the arm. 'Señora,' she says confidentially and I can feel myself bristling with anger. She's going to split on us, the little sneak. Then she whispers to Miss Martínez, just loud enough for us all to hear, 'Jaime is embarrassed by her purchase. She has not spent much on her mother's present. Let me take you to a stall that sells better quality goods.'

She moves off with Miss Martínez who is completely taken in by her. I am left with burning cheeks, unsure whether to feel grateful to her for her quick actions or totally insulted by her dissing of my carefully chosen present for my mum in front of everyone.

By the time I've handed the chicks safely back to Jason, it's all academic anyway. I can't give that tablecloth to anyone. Whatever the quality.

The chicks have pooed all over it.

But there are worse things that can happen.

If only we could have gone back to England at that point. Concha and I could have been almost-friends. It wasn't to be though. And it was all Tira's fault.

That night the school holds a farewell disco for the British exchange kids. It's meant to be just for us and our partners, but when Señor Gómez drops us off, there are loads of kids hanging about outside, trying to get in on the action. Goodness knows why.

Inside it's no different from home: 1980s compilations belting out; female teachers dancing self-consciously in the middle, trying unsuccessfully to get the kids to join in; male teachers, looking like they've been hired by Securicor for the night, telling off the boys who are sliding about on their knees on the polished floor; girls dressed up to look hot but frozen with boredom. My heart sinks. What is it about a school disco that makes boys act like six-year-olds and girls feel about ninety?

Concha, beside me, lets out a big sigh. She looks great tonight, in tight jeans and high heels that elongate her legs, and a yellow bodice with a lacy trim that makes her look more girly than usual. She'd had her hair beaded at the market and it suits her off her face, making her eyes with their impressive lashes stand out. I don't blame her for choosing to hang out with the older kids. She's far too old for this lot.

Actually, I'm feeling pretty mature myself, I don't feel like me. I've decided to dress up tonight, since it's my last night in Spain, in a strapless white mini-dress I bought at the market. It's the most daring thing I've ever owned and I don't know what Mum's going to say when she sees it, but it looks fabulous against my newly-tanned skin, with my hair down around my shoulders. Because I'm in flats and Concha's in heels, we're more on a par, height-wise, than normal.

'Let's get a drink,' she says.

Miss Martínez and Señor Hairy Ears, who I've since discovered is actually called Señor Jiminez (I now know you pronounce the Spanish J like our H . . . anyway, he'll always be Hairy Ears to me), are doling out plastic cups full of Coke. 'What, no Bacardi?' asks Concha and Miss Martínez laughs but I don't think Concha is joking and neither does old Hairy Ears because he gives her what my mum calls an old-fashioned look. We move across to the dance floor and stare glumly at Adam, Jason, Nacho and Sergio, who are doing a pathetic version of the Moonwalk in tune with the 1980s music belting from the speakers.

'This is rubbish,' she says. 'Come with me.'

I take a look around for Fern or Holly but there's no sign of them so I follow her meekly to the loo. Inside, she extracts a bottle from her bag and takes a swig, then offers it to me.

'What is it?'

'Just a liqueur thing my grandmother uses in cooking. Try it.'

I do as she says. It's sweet, thick and cloying and makes me shudder.

'It's better with Coke,' says Concha and pours some into my cup.

'Steady!' I take a cautious sip, then another bigger one. It's not so bad now; Coke with a bit of bite to it.

'Got to have something to make this evening rock!' she grins.

I'm not so sure about that, but it's nice to see Concha in a good mood and looking after me so I smile back at her and raise my plastic glass. She clicks hers against mine and we both take another drink.

'Dance?' I say, a bit worried that I'm going to get drunk if I'm not careful.

'Sure,' she says and knocks back the rest of her glass. 'After you.'

I lead the way on to the dance floor and I don't know

if it's the drink or because it's my last night in Spain or just that Concha and I are friends at last, but I really throw myself into dancing and let myself go. Concha and I have a real laugh, twirling each other around, doing take-offs of dances from the Eighties to match the music, and when Fern and Dolores turn up they join in, and so do Holly and Ana. Soon there's a load of us rocking around on the dance floor and everyone is watching us. Tonight I don't mind being the centre of attention at all. It's fun.

Do you know something, I think I've changed. I don't know what's happened to nervous, shy little Jaime. Mum is going to have such a surprise when I get home. No more Wilma Worryguts! I'm Tira now!

'Tira!' I shout in time to the music, flinging my arms wide, and everyone laughs and copies me.

'Tira!' they shout back with their arms in the air. It's brilliant.

It's thirsty work though, all this dancing, so Concha, who's being really lovely tonight, goes off and comes back with a tray of Cokes for us all. I knock mine back gratefully and take another one.

'Having fun?' she asks.

'You bet!' Impulsively I throw my arms around her and give her a hug. I feel full of warmth and love. 'I'm going to miss you!'

'Me too!' she says and hugs me back. 'But don't worry. I'm coming to stay with you in the summer!'

'I can't wait!'

'Come on!'

'Where are we going? Wait for me!'

She's off so fast I stumble as I try to keep up with her. Thank goodness I'm wearing flats. Outside, the air has cooled down and most of the kids who were trying to gatecrash have given up and gone home. There's just a group of older kids left under the streetlamp, some of them on scooters. Concha makes a beeline for them so I follow her, though for some reason my feet don't seem to want to walk in a beeline, they want to walk in a wavy line. It must have been all that dancing I've been doing. It seems really funny to me how my feet have developed a mind of their own and I start giggling. A couple of the boys glance up and their faces break into a grin.

'Pablo!' I say wildly and throw my arms wide. 'Eduardo! My friends!' What has got into me?

Pablo says, 'Hi!' and stretches his arms out and I fall into them and kiss him, first on one cheek, then on the other, the Spanish way. He stares at me, as if he's surprised to find me quite so friendly.

Actually, I'd like to kiss him on the lips.

'Are you OK, Jaime?' he asks and too late I realize he was putting his arms out to steady me, not kiss me. But for some reason, tonight I don't care.

'I'm not Jaime, I'm Tira,' I say, by way of explanation, and let Jaime submerge and my mad side take over. I put my head back and laugh out loud at his startled expression. And then my ankle decides it doesn't want to support me any longer and I stumble again and this time he grabs me by the arm before I fall.

'You have been drinking?' he asks, but it's a question not a statement, so I shake my head.

'Not really. Only a bit of Coke with something Concha put in it,' I say, surprised myself by the effect it's having on me. Then I remember what my mum always says and change it to, 'I mean, a drop of Coke. A drop. Drop,' I repeat, seeing his puzzled face. 'We say, a drop for liquids, a bit for solids.'

'What?' He looks bewildered.

'I'm giving you an English lesson. D R O P. Drop. You wanted me to give you English lessons, remember? Oops,' My ankle turns again and I clutch his arm. He moves it round my waist to steady me. 'That's nice,' I say. 'My legs are all wobbly tonight. Wibbly-wobbly. Wibber-ly-wobb-er-ly. How do you say that in Spanish?'

He looks confused. He's so good-looking. I can see what Concha sees in him. 'Tell me!' I say bossily, then I giggle. I'm never bossy normally, it must be Tira at work. 'I don't want to go back to England not knowing the

115

Spanish word for wibbly-wobbly.'

His eyes crinkle up in amusement. *'¡Piripi!'* he says. *'Estás piripi.'*

'What's that mean?' I gaze up at him with affection from the safety of his arms. I really like Pablo.

'You are drunk, that's what that means!' says Concha, appearing from nowhere, her brows drawn together in an angry straight line when she sees me in Pablo's arms.

'No I'm not, I'm . . . wibbly-wobbly,' I protest, but actually I think she might be right. Everything is starting to whirl around and I feel dizzy.

'Piripi,' repeats Pablo, grinning at Concha. 'What have you done to her?'

'Yo?' Concha's eyebrows separate and rise innocently up into her hairline. 'Me? Nothing.'

'She needs to go home.'

'No!' I protest feebly. 'I'm having fun.' But actually, I'm lying. I'm fed up with Tira now. I wish she'd shut up or disappear. I'm starting to feel tired and queasy and I don't like the way the world is spinning around me. None of this is fun any more. I just want to go home to bed. I lurch away from the others and sink down on to the kerb; my head drops between my knees and I allow Tira to drain away.

'Take me home,' I moan. I'm scared I'm going to puke up in front of everyone.

'I don't want to go home yet,' snaps Concha.

'Please,' I say feebly.

Concha curses under her breath. Pablo raps out something to her in Spanish and she answers back sulkily. He looks cross, then he says, in English, 'OK then. Jaime? I will take you home.'

'No!' squeals Concha, changing her mind quickly. 'You give *me* a lift home. Jaime can go with Eduardo.'

I look up. Eduardo shakes his head vehemently. I don't think he's too keen on the idea. Pablo sighs, pulls his helmet on and stretches out a hand to me. 'Come on.' I grasp it and he hauls me up and helps me on to the back of his scooter, making sure I'm wedged tight against the pillion. 'Here!' He takes my bag which is dangling from my hand and places it safely over my head and across my body. 'Now it is safe!' he says and I smile back at him weakly. He's so kind. 'Hold tight,' he says and gets on in front of me. I wrap my arms obediently around him and rest my head gratefully on the warm, solid surface of his back. Concha glares at me, then leaps on to the back of Eduardo's scooter. 'See you at home,' she growls as she roars off into the night.

Even in my befuddled state, I know I shouldn't be doing this. Miss Martínez warned and warned us of the dangers of scooters before we came out to Spain. I haven't even got a crash helmet. But Pablo kicks the engine into life and we lurch forward, me hanging on to him desperately. He avoids the main roads and we drive through the dark back streets, skidding on the cobbles but somehow managing to avoid the people who emerge from lighted doorways, the parked cars, the rubbish bags piled up for the morning, the fleeting shadows of cats. I clutch on to him tightly, partly to keep warm, partly to stop myself sliding off. After a while, Pablo pulls up, places his feet on the ground and turns around, pushing his visor up.

'OK?'

I nod my head even though it's not true. I'm not OK, I feel cold and decidedly unwell and I just want to get home to bed.

'Not far now. Do you want to get off, walk around a little? How do you say? Sober up, before you go home?'

Sounds like a good idea. I can't face Señor Gómez and Abuela like this. I nod again and try to get off the scooter, but it's more difficult than I thought. My dress is too tight and my legs don't want to cooperate. Maybe I can just slide off.

'Whoa!' says Pablo. 'Wait. I will help you.'

He parks up the bike and takes his helmet off, then he lifts me down, his hands under my armpits.

'Thanks.' He holds on to me, making sure I'm steady, and I smile up at him gratefully. He smiles back, his mouth curling up attractively. I can't take my eyes off it. Suddenly, before I even know what I'm doing, I reach up and press my lips to his. He looks surprised for a second, as surprised as I am, then he kisses me back.

Who would have thought it? Shy little Jaime! Her first kiss, and it's under a Mediterranean moon, from a really hot guy, with a sexy Spanish accent.

But it's not Jaime, is it? Concha spiked her drinks and now it's Tira who's taken over and is leading the way and Pablo, who can't believe his luck, is responding.

It's all happening so fast . . . too fast . . . she's dizzy with it all. Her world is spinning round and round whirling, swirling, out of control . . .

. . . And then she was sick.

I don't want to go into detail. It was awful.

I wasn't sick over him!

Well, I was over his shoes.

Then I moved over to hang on to the wall and I was
sick there too.

After that, I disappeared down an alley and was sick for
a third time.

It was, without doubt, the worst moment of my life.

Afterwards, I immediately feel better. In a physical way
that is. On the other hand, mentally, I'm disorientated
and confused, and emotionally, I'm wrecked. I am so
embarrassed . . . no, appalled . . . no, totally mortified . . .
by what has happened that I want to run as far away as
possible from the awful scene of crime.

Not the most sensible thing to do perhaps. But I do it anyway.

I can hear Pablo calling my name but I stumble off down the alleyway, away from his voice. It's pitch-black, the moon hidden behind high buildings, and I can't see where I'm going. The next minute, I topple over what appears to be a dustbin, banging my shins in the process. There's a loud clatter as the lid falls off and rolls away down the lane and every dog in the neighbourhood starts barking. In a house behind me, an angry voice yells and a light is switched on. I pick myself up and run, hell for leather, through the twisting, narrow alleyways, away from the shouts, from Pablo, from everything, till I can run no more.

When I finally stop, I can hardly breathe and I'm totally lost. I bend over, retching again, but this time there is nothing left to bring up (sorry, too much information) and I sink down with my back against a wall, utterly drained, and wait for my heartbeat to return to normal.

I don't know where I am.

I feel so ashamed.

Tears course down my face. Mum? I need you.

Around me, silent backs of buildings stand shoulder to shoulder, some tall and forbidding, others hunched over with disapproval, in this graveyard of a place. The darkness steals around me like a corpse, clinging to my skin with shrivelled fingers, and I shiver in the cold night air. It's really creepy here. Something rustles and I shriek as what *must* be a rat skitters past me and disappears down the lane. Leaping to my feet, I flee, back the way I came, back to light, people, Pablo.

I wish.

Everything looks different. At the top, the lane branches in two and I take the left-hand fork, thinking that's the way I'd come. But it seems to go on for ever. I must have made a mistake, so I race back down and up the other side, only I'm not sure that's right either, because I don't recognize a thing. I fight down the panic rising in my throat like bile and keep going, slower now because I can't keep the pace up, keeping to the middle of the lane, avoiding the shrouded edges. When there is a choice of turnings I make them arbitrarily, left-right, right-left, because what does it matter, I haven't got a clue where I am, as I make my way like a terrified lab rat through the maze of alleys.

And all the time, I'm jumping at the night noises, the yowls and scuttles and creaks and rattles, and flinching at the shifts and shapes in the shadows. But most of all, I'm pleading, non-stop, in the darkness, 'Please let me get home safely. Please let me get home safely,' over and over again, until, at last, my prayers are answered. Ahead of me, I see a light and I run towards it and before long I'm back in the night world I know, of streetlights and cars and people, though there is no sign of Pablo.

I don't wait around to look for him. He's probably gone home, furious with me. I wouldn't blame him. But I don't even know if this is the place where we stopped. I didn't notice to be honest, I had other things on my mind then. I block out the memory of that kiss and breathe a sigh of relief as I realize my bag is still draped over my shoulder. Pablo did that for me. Even if he didn't hang around, at least I have him to thank for making sure I've got the means to get home. I recall him placing it gently over my head and tears threaten to engulf me. I scrub my eyes furiously. Just get yourself home, Jaime.

I follow the lights to the main road where people are spilling out of bars and clubs and into taxis. And I've taken out my purse to see if I've got enough money on me to get one when I suddenly realize that buses are still running and I've got my pass with me. I join the queue, aware that I'm attracting a bit of attention in my strapless dress which is no longer white nor elegant, and I don't need anyone to tell me my hair and face is a mess, but I give everyone my best scowl, modelled on Concha's, and ignore them. On the bus I do a quick repair job, wiping off the mascara run, adding a bit of blusher and lippy to bring colour back to my pinched face and combing my hair. Then I smooth down my dress with my hands, brushing off the dirt I'd managed to gather on my mad rampage through back alleys and finally spritz myself with perfume. There.

It all seems surreal now, like it happened to someone else.

Thank goodness I'm going home in the morning.

When I get off the bus, I walk quickly to Concha's, wondering how on earth I'm going to get in. A car goes past with some boys hanging out of the window, whistling and shouting at me, but I ignore them and they drive on. Then a guy on a motorbike slows down behind me and says something but I ignore him too, keeping my eyes firmly ahead. What is it with these Spanish guys, can't they take no for an answer? When I reach the apartment block, he pulls in too and I glance at him, partly in alarm, partly in exasperation, and realize belatedly it's a scooter, not a motorbike, and it's Pablo. I come to a halt as his bike stops beside me and he sits astride it, his feet on the road.

'Are you OK?'

I nod, too embarrassed to look him in the eye, but then I notice I'm staring right at his shoes which still look a bit splattered so I glance up quickly and find him looking at me.

'Why did you run away? I could not find you! I looked for you everywhere.'

'I'm sorry.'

'I was worried. I was afraid you would not get home.'

'I did. I'm fine.'

I feel terrible. What a liability he must think I am. First he sees me home, even though I'm nothing to him, because I'm too . . . *piripi* to make it myself: then I snog him and things get really hot; then I puke all over his shoes; then I run off like a demented chicken. Tomorrow it will be all round the school.

'I don't know how I'm going to get in,' I gulp, glancing up at the third floor.

'Easy. Some stones?' He points to the road and I bend down and pass a handful to him. He lobs one at Concha's window, not even bothering to get off his bike. I can hear it's met its target. Something tells me he's done this before. He does it again. And again. The next second, the window opens and Concha's head appears.

'Let me in!' I call up to her. Concha stares down at us both for a minute then says, 'I'll open the door,' before her head disappears and the window closes.

I look back at Pablo. 'I'd better go,' I say in relief as I hear the buzzer. The door opens and, before he can say anything, I slip through it quickly. It swings shut behind me. The last thing I see before I disappear round the corner to the lift is his surprised face looking over the handlebars of his scooter. As the lift bears me up to the third floor I think, I bet he's glad to see the back of me.

Upstairs, Concha is at the front door of the flat with her finger to her lips. I tiptoe behind her in to her darkened bedroom, shut the door and collapse on to my bed, closing my eyes in relief, glad to have avoided a confrontation. She didn't need to tell me to be quiet, the last thing I want to do is waken Señor Gómez and Abuela.

'Do you know what time it is?' A fierce whisper penetrates the darkness and suddenly the light is snapped on. My eyes spring open in shock. Concha towers above me, hands on her hips, glowering.

'What?'

'Where do you think you've been till this time?'

I swallow and struggle to sit up. I expected to have this conversation one day, but strangely I thought it would be with my mother.

'I've been coming home . . . with Pablo . . .'

'I know you've been with Pablo. Look at the state of you! You look as if you've been rolling about on the ground.'

I glance down guiltily at my once-white dress. I thought I'd managed to brush off the dirt, but now I can see it still looks decidedly grubby. No wonder; I *have* been rolling on the ground, but with a dustbin, not Pablo. I open my mouth to explain but Concha jumps in first.

'What took you so long?'

'We stopped . . .' I lick my lips which have mysteriously become very dry. 'Just for a bit.'

'For a bit? More like for hours!' She takes a step closer. 'I've been back ages!' she says, jabbing an accusing finger in my face. Involuntarily I shrink away from her. 'What did you stop for?'

What can I say? To vomit at his feet? She'd love that.

'Just to talk,' I say feebly.

'Talk!' she sneers. 'Do you think I'm stupid?' She pushes her face up to mine, so close I can smell the sweet, cloying liqueur still clinging to her breath. She's probably been drinking more of it while she's been sitting here waiting for me to come home. I'm scared but I'm angry as well. It's all her fault. If she hadn't spiked my drink, none of this would've happened.

'You snogged him, didn't you?' she says venomously.

'No I didn't!' I lie, but I go red and she can tell.

'Yes you did!' She stares at me in surprise as if she didn't really believe it herself till this minute. 'You kissed him.'

'It wasn't like that . . .'

'Bitch!' she says and turns away, but not before I see tears forming in her eyes. 'If you think I'm coming to stay with you in the summer, you've got another thing coming!'

'Concha, let me explain,' I say but she hisses something horrible at me and snaps off the light and I shut up.

I lie there feeling terrible, the events of the night churning round and round in my head. Being sick after your first kiss is bad enough, but cheating on a friend is worse.

And it doesn't matter how much I tell myself that Concha is not a friend, in fact she's evil: she never wanted me here in the first place . . . *and* she spiked my drink . . . *and* she threw my books around the classroom . . . *and* she made me look stupid at the procession . . . *and* she ran off and abandoned me countless times . . . none of it makes a blind bit of difference.

The fact is, you don't cheat on your mates, whether you like them or not. And Concha was my exchange mate. We'd *chosen* each other, even if we'd both got it badly wrong. Now I knew she would never make that return visit to England and for some inexplicable reason that made me very sad. It was my fault, not hers. I *knew* Concha regarded Pablo as her property but I snogged him anyway. And tomorrow, when he spreads the word around school and everyone knows the whole sorry tale, the Spanish kids will all have a good laugh about it.

And it didn't help at all to know they'd be laughing at Concha too, because they hated her. That only made it worse.

How could I have got things so wrong?

My one consolation was that I wouldn't be there to deal with it. We were leaving first thing in the morning. And I would never, *ever* have to see Concha or Pablo again.

It's a rush in the morning. I wake up late with a throbbing headache and groan as the memory of last night floods back. I turn over to see Concha's bed is empty. What a relief. Quickly I pack my case with one eye on the clock, pulling my clothes from the wardrobe, emptying the drawers. My dress I roll into a ball and stuff in the bottom of my case.

'Concha's gone for a run,' says Señor Gómez, looking pretty astonished at his daughter's sudden desire to get fit. 'She'll be back soon. I told her what time you need to leave for the airport.'

I sit in the sunny kitchen and try to eat breakfast with Abuela for the last time, but all I can manage is a drink of water. She thinks I am sad because I am going and she gives me a present. It's a black crocheted shawl, beautiful and delicate as lace, though I can't ever see me wearing it.

'For Mama,' she says, noting my surprise, and I nod in understanding. 'For you,' she adds simply and hands me a small, square-shaped parcel wrapped in tissue paper.

'Open it later,' says Señor Gómez, coming in and checking his watch against the clock. 'We must leave now or we will miss the plane.'

I give Abuela a fierce hug. There is nothing of her; her shoulder blades jut through her flesh like a wire coat hanger. Tears fall off the end of her long nose as she steps back and thrusts a brown bag into my hands.

'Tapas,' explains her son. 'She made them for you last night.'

'*Gracias,* Abuela,' I say, then I start crying as well.

'Tapas and tears,' Señor Gómez scoffs, but he looks sad too. His mother's case stands ready in the hall. She will be leaving later today to return home now her work looking after me is done. He and Concha will be left alone in the flat. 'Where is Concha?' he barks. 'We cannot wait. We will have to go without her.'

That's fine by me. Downstairs we place my bag in the boot of Señor Gómez's car and I sit next to him in the front and wave goodbye to Abuela, bent double as she peers into the car, fluttering a white lace handkerchief. When I look back at her through the rear window, I see the hanky is pressed to her face.

I also see Concha, arms folded, scowl in place, leaning

against the wall of the apartment block, round the corner from the entrance. She cuts a lonely figure. Silently, I raise my hand in farewell, but she turns away.

At the airport, most people are already there along with their exchange partners and their families. It's so noisy! Everyone is excited, jabbering away like mad, swapping phone numbers, email addresses and internet site details, promising to keep in touch, making crazy plans for the return visit to the UK later in the term. Miss Martínez is running around counting heads; Señor Gómez looks at her with interest but she is too busy to notice him.

'What happened to you last night?' asks Fern and I shrug and say, 'Went home,' and she turns back to console Dolores who is so distraught you'd swear she was about to die by lethal injection, rather than say goodbye to her exchange partner. Ana's just as bad, wrapped around Holly like a python. I sigh. Where's my fan club? I glance up at Señor Gómez, standing stiffly beside me.

'You can go if you like,' I say. 'No need to wait.'

He brightens up. 'Are you sure?' He kisses my cheeks then hesitates and places his hands on my shoulders. His eyes are soft. 'I am sorry about Concha,' he says gently. 'She is difficult, I know. But things have not been easy for her.'

I don't know what to say.

'You have been very good to her,' he says. 'Very kind. Your mother would be proud of you.'

No she wouldn't. I feel myself going red. I thought I'd got over that, but my guilty conscience is catching me out.

'She likes you, you know,' he continues. 'She is looking forward to coming to the UK to stay with you.'

How wrong can you be? I stare at him glumly, wondering if I should confess all. Something tells me he really wouldn't want to hear it. He smiles at me again, does his funny little clicky thing, looks vainly in Miss Martínez's direction, and takes his leave.

I don't have time to dwell on feeling sad or bad because the next second it's all goodbyes and we're being ushered through Departures. First of all we have our hand luggage checked. It's much stricter than on the ferry; they make us take our shoes off and empty our pockets. We put our stuff into trays and watch as they move along a conveyor belt with our bags to be examined on an X-ray machine.

'What are they looking for?' asks Fern, wide-eyed.

'Drugs? Knives? Stuff to blow up the plane?' says Holly who's been to Florida with her parents (when they were still together) and knows about these things. It's funny, I immediately go bright red even though I wouldn't know an illegal substance if it stood up and bit me in the face and I certainly have no intention of bombing the plane, I just want it to get me home again as soon as possible. I look so guilty I'm sure they're going to arrest me.

They don't take any notice of me though. They're far too busy examining Jason's tray with expressions of disbelief on their faces. Guess what they found in it, even though he'd tried to hide it under his hoody? A walking, squawking, very indignant grey duckling that didn't think much of being dumped in a tray with Jason's smelly clothes draped over its head. Then, lo and behold, one sleepy gecko is discovered in Adam's bag, wrapped up nice and warm in his underwear, and, when he steps through the gate, two fluffy chicks are found in his pockets. They give the game away by cheeping appreciatively when the security guard runs his wand down the outside of Adam's jeans. It's surprising how much they've grown in one day! Next minute, Jason and Adam are marched away for a full body search. I don't know where else they think they might have secreted some creatures, but they're taking no chances, that's for sure. Miss Martínez and Mr Evans have a frenzied conversation and start making frantic phone calls to school.

In the end they let them get on the plane with the rest of us. I think they must have given them a really good telling-off because I've never seem them so subdued. In fact, once the excitement of take-off is over, everyone quietens down. Next to me, Fern scans through the duty-free magazine and beyond her, Holly puts her seat back and falls asleep. I'm next to the window and I rest my aching brow against the cool glass and gaze out at the clear blue sky as we fly over Spain and France, back to England.

The holiday is over. We're going home.

Two months later

Miss Martínez moves around the classroom, placing a letter in front of certain people, talking non-stop as she goes.

'OK, those of you who went on the exchange trip, listen up. As you know, your partners will be arriving tomorrow. All the information you need is contained in this letter. It tells you when they will be arriving at school and I don't have to remind you to be there on time to greet them; it's got a list of the trips you will be accompanying them on and details of . . .'

Her voice gallops ahead, steering us through the steeplechase of exchange information, but I'd already come to a halt at the first, insurmountable hurdle. Concha would be arriving tomorrow to stay with me for practically a fortnight. Thirteen days and twelve nights of Concepción Inmaculada, 24/7. How was I going to stand it?

I've been dreading this. The exchange partner from hell. *She* wasn't there to greet *me* when I arrived in Spain, was she? I'd a good mind not to meet her, let *her* see what it feels like to arrive in a foreign country for the first time and be totally abandoned.

To tell the truth, I was surprised she was even coming; the last thing she ever said to me was that she would definitely not be making the return visit.

I was so mortified when I got back from Spain. I felt awful about the whole Pablo episode, I knew I'd behaved really badly and let myself and Concha down and was sure I'd made myself a real laughing-stock. But once I was home and a few days had passed, and I'd caught up on my sleep, it didn't seem so terrible after all. Nobody here knew what I'd done and I'd checked the internet sites and found nothing dreadful had been posted about me in Spain, thank goodness, just a few disco photos of me (or rather, Tira!) dancing crazily; not just me, I hasten to add, the other girls were as well!

It was Concha's fault anyway. I'd never have kissed Pablo and got myself into such a crazy situation if she hadn't doctored my drink.

Would I?

Anyway, it had all died a death and I'd stopped agonizing about it ages ago, burying it in the deepest recess of my mind. But now, even though I hadn't heard a dicky-bird from my exchange partner over the past couple of months, it was all about to be resurrected. I had to assume, because I'd heard nothing to the contrary, that she *was* coming after all.

Payback time.

'Any other questions?'

I switch back to the present and look down at my desk. Then I put my hand up.

'Jaime?'

'You didn't give me a letter, Miss.'

'Nor me.'

'Oh, Jaime, Adam, I'm sorry. I meant to tell you. I'm afraid your exchange partners aren't coming.'

My heart misses a beat.

'Why not?' asks Adam, blank with shock.

'Ignacio had an accident yesterday playing football. He's broken his leg.'

A groan echoes round the classroom and poor Adam bangs the desk in disappointment. We all like Nacho.

'What about Concha, Miss?' asks Fern.

'Um . . . I'm not sure.' Miss Martínez looks a bit awkward, like she's sorry for me. 'I think she just decided she didn't want to come. I'm sorry, Jaime.'

Everyone looks at me, probably expecting me to flush bright red with embarrassment. Let's face it, it is a tad humiliating when your exchange partner refuses to pay you a return visit. So she's not coming after all? I feel like a two-ton weight has been lifted from my shoulders.

'I didn't want her anyway!' I shrug and the class cheers.

Miss Martínez frowns at me. 'That's not the spirit of exchange.'

'You try exchanging with Loopy Gómez López, Miss!' remarks Holly.

I lower my head, avoiding my teacher's gaze. I know that was a horrible thing to say. I've changed. I've got tougher. I had to! Exchange did that to me and I guess I've got Concha partly to thank for it. Whenever she's needed, like now, Tira Tough-Nut comes back to save the day.

The trouble is, I'm not quite sure I like the new me. And judging by her disapproving look, I think Miss Martínez might feel the same.

When I tell Mum that Concha's decided not to come after all, we end up having a row.

We've had a lot of rows lately.

I don't think Mum thinks much of the new me either.

As it happens, I don't like the new her.

Exchange didn't just make me change; it allowed her to as well.

I didn't want my mum to change, I preferred her the way she was.

* * *

142

When I came through Arrivals at the airport, I didn't recognize her at first. I suppose I was on the alert for a middle-aged, dumpyish woman with untidy, mousy hair, wearing a pair of old trousers and her familiar green fleecy. Well, I wouldn't tell her that's what she looked like, obviously, but it's a pretty good description, believe me. Or it was. And I was expecting to see her in the middle of a crowd of mums having a gossip or on her own waiting patiently.

I walked straight past her. She was standing to one side, talking to Holly's dad, and I suppose they looked like a couple so I didn't even glance at them. Then I heard Mum's voice say, 'Jaime?' and I stopped and nearly did a double-take. No wonder I didn't recognize her. She'd had her hair cut, all soft and feathery, and it had been highlighted too. It took years off her. And she was wearing jeans and a long, loose top which made her look loads slimmer.

'Mum!' I squealed. 'You look fantastic! I love your hair!' I did too, at that moment. I still do actually, it really suits her; it's the other stuff I don't like. 'You've lost weight! Have you been eating properly?'

'I'm supposed to be asking you that,' Mum laughed and crushed me to her. 'I've missed you.'

'I've missed you too!' I said, squeezing her tight. Phew! She still felt like the same old mum, soft and squashy, beneath the cool clothes and the highlights. Bliss! I think everyone felt the same at the airport, glad to be home again; we were all milling round, hugging our parents, like we'd come out of a long afternoon at nursery school to find them waiting at the gate to take us home for tea, bath and bed.

It was nice when we got home too. Mum had made me my favourite fish pie with cheesy potato on top (nursery food!) and afterwards we curled up on the sofa together with my old quilt over us and ate the chocolates I'd bought for her in place of the chick-polluted tablecloth. Then I gave her the tablecloth anyway and told her the chicks-duckling-gecko saga and she laughed her head off and said, 'Not to worry, it'll wash. It's *very* good quality.'

Concha Gómez, eat your heart out!

It was lovely sitting there together, sipping tea which I hadn't had for a fortnight, eating chocolates and swapping news.

'I've signed up for Spanish lessons,' she said. 'Thought I could give you a hand with your GCSE.'

'Great!' I said and told her all about the exchange. Well, not *all* about the exchange, obviously; there were some things I preferred to keep to myself. She was so interested in everything and asked me loads of questions and I told her as much as I could.

'You sound as if you had a wonderful time,' she said triumphantly, 'I knew you'd enjoy it!' and when I thought about it I had to admit to myself that, on the whole, I had. Then Mum poured me a bath, full to the brim with bubbles, and afterwards I felt really tired and sleepy so I went straight to bed and snuggled down. Tea, bath and bed! Whether you're four or fourteen, it's the nicest feeling in the world to be looked after by your mum. It makes you feel . . . cherished.

Poor Concha. She didn't have a mum to cherish her. But she had Abuela.

I sat up in bed. How could I have forgotten! I had a present from Abuela that I hadn't looked at yet! And one for Mum! I found them in my case; leaving mine on the bed, I went downstairs in search of Mum.

She was on the phone in the lounge. I could hear her laughing as I pushed the door open. She looked up startled and said into the phone, 'Just a minute, Jaime's here,' then cradled the receiver in her hand. 'Yes, sweetheart? What do you want?'

I held out the present to her. 'I forgot. This is for you. From Abuela.'

'Thanks. Just put it there.' She indicated the table. I put it down and waited. 'Anything else?' she asked.

'No.'

'I'll be up to say goodnight in a minute.' She smiled at

me blandly, obviously waiting for me to go so she could continue her conversation.

'OK.' I went back upstairs to my bedroom, puzzled.

Who was she on the phone to at this time of night?

Someone I knew, that's for sure. 'Jaime's here,' she'd said.

So why was it so private?

On my bed lay my present from Abuela. I got into bed and opened it. Inside was a framed photo of Concha aged about seven or eight. I'd seen it before, but where? Then it came to me: on the wall in Abuela's bedroom, only a much bigger version. Now I recognized what it was: a photograph of Concha's First Holy Communion. She was wearing a very ornate long white dress, clasping a prayer book in her white-gloved hands and smiling proudly into the camera. Her hair was arranged in neat ringlets beneath a veil and a tiara. Behind her stood a younger-looking Señor Gómez and a beautiful, well-groomed woman. Concha looked so happy and innocent, like a tiny, bashful bride.

How could anyone change so much? I felt a lump in my throat. Carefully I placed the photo on my bedside table, switched off the light and lay down in bed, drawing the duvet up round my ears.

Downstairs I could hear Mum still droning on. Who was she talking to all this time for goodness sake?

So much for missing me! At last it went silent and after a while she appeared clasping the shawl at my bedroom door.

'Jaime? Jaime?' she whispered. 'Are you awake?'

I didn't answer. She could've been talking to me for the past fifteen minutes if she'd wanted to, only she'd preferred to continue her telephone conversation with mystery mate on the end of the line. Stuff her.

'It's beautiful,' she said, but I pretended to be asleep.

I think that's when the rot started with Mum, that night. I was peeved and you can't blame me. I'd been away for a fortnight and *she* preferred to yack on the phone to someone she could talk to any old time rather than come and say goodnight to me. I was the one who was supposed to be glued to the phone all the time, not her.

Or maybe it was the next morning when she found my grubby, screwed-up, once-white dress at the bottom of my case and gave me the third degree about it.

Either way, now I was home again, things seemed a bit different somehow, a bit skewed. Like for some reason I no longer felt I was the total centre of Mum's universe. I was still high priority, but I wasn't completely pivotal, if you know what I mean. I was no longer the apple of my mother's eye.

The funny thing was that, before I went on that exchange, I didn't even realize I was. I knew I was pretty important to her, all right. I knew she worked hard to make us a decent living; I knew she'd always make sure she was home at the same time every night to cook my dinner for me; I knew she did all the shopping and the washing and the cleaning and if I needed anything, she'd get it; I knew every day she would ask me about school and friends and teachers, help me with my homework, check my life was running smoothly. But I never worked out that her whole life revolved around me until it stopped. I guess I took it all for granted. That's what mums do and actually, it can get a bit too much when you feel that you are the sole focus of their attention.

I mean, we got on well before, but sometimes I used to wish, get a life, Mum.

But nowadays we row all the time.

Because, that's exactly what Mum did.

She got a life.

And I don't like it one bit.

'What do you mean, she's not coming?'

I shrug.

'Why not?'

'I don't know.'

'Is she ill?'

'No. Miss Martínez says she doesn't want to. That's all I know.'

'She can't just change her mind like that.'

I snort. 'She can. You don't know Concha. She's a law unto herself.'

'But I've got everything ready!' She gestures helplessly towards the spare room, normally chock-a-block with junk, now clean, tidy and inviting with its new bedspread and rug and empty drawers. 'I spent the whole weekend clearing this out,' she mutters. 'Never mind the expense!'

'It's not my fault!' I protest, but of course it is.

'Why didn't you tell me before? I've got all this

shopping in!' She opens the fridge door and inspects the contents glumly. There's enough there to feed a family for a fortnight.

Which is precisely what she thought she was going to do.

'I only knew yesterday. And you were out last night, remember?'

She has the grace to look abashed. 'It was only my evening class.'

Yeah, right. When I was in Spain she decided to learn Spanish herself so she enrolled at an evening class. Like why? My disgust must have shown in my face because she says crossly, 'Anyway, you could've told me when you were having your tea.'

'You were upstairs getting ready.'

'And afterwards?'

'I was doing my homework.'

So busy doing my homework that I didn't even bother to raise my head when she'd said, 'I'm off now, Jaime. Is there anything you want?'

The truth was, I didn't trust myself to answer. Because if I had I would've said, 'Yes, I want you to stay in with me like you used to, instead of going to stupid evening classes.'

Because the thing is, I'm not convinced she is going to Spanish classes, not dressed up to the nines like that.

She looks more like she's going out on the pull.

Don't go there.

So I just grunted when she'd said, 'Mrs Bick's here.' Because that's another thing. *She's* too old to be . . . doing whatever she's doing . . . and *I'm* too old to be babysat.

'You could've told me when I came in.'

'It was late. I was asleep.' A lie, on both counts, and she knows it. 'Anyway,' I add sullenly. 'If you didn't waste money on a babysitter for me, you'd have more money to pay for food.'

For a second she looks as if she wants to slap me but instead she takes a deep breath and says, 'Never mind, it can't be helped. See you tonight.'

She moves forward to give me a kiss, but I turn my head away swiftly and have the satisfaction of glimpsing the hurt expression in her eyes. Serves her right. I'm not going to let my mother send me on a guilt trip. She's the one who should be feeling guilty, not me. Packs me off on an exchange trip and no sooner am I out of the way than she's got off with someone. I know she has, though she denies it. She must have been biding her time, waiting for this opportunity for years. And all the time, I thought we were happy, just the two of us.

'Bye, Jaime,' she says and the door bangs shut behind her. She's gone. My warm glow of satisfaction drains away, melting my anger into a turgid, slimy ooze in the pit of my stomach. I feel sick. I want to run after her and fling my arms around her before it's too late and say, 'I'm sorry!' But if I do, then she'll think I'm OK with whatever she's doing and carry on.

I hate her.

I wish I'd never been on the flipping exchange in the first place.

Which reminds me! The Spanish kids are arriving today! It would be nice to see Dolores and Ana and Sergio and everyone again. I grab my bag and head out of the door for school, feeling better already.

That afternoon I'm allowed off the last lesson to wait outside school with the other exchangees for the Spanish kids to arrive. Everyone is so excited. Most people have stayed in contact with their partners and become real friends. I start to feel a bit jealous when I listen to Fern going on, not because I'm possessive of her (well, I am, though it's OK, I like Dolores as well), but because I find myself wishing my partner was coming too.

'What? Concha?' says Fern, her jaw dropping when I confess this to her.

'Yeah, I do.' I've surprised myself. 'She wasn't that bad really. I mean, we were beginning to get along OK in the end.' Until I mucked up, I add to myself silently.

'No accounting for taste! You've had a lucky escape if

you ask me. It's tough on Adam though. He's gutted Nacho can't come.'

I glance over at Adam, kicking a football round with the boys. He didn't look gutted to me, he looked quite happy. Boys are different from girls, no question. They're not so ruled by their feelings.

'Bus!' yells Holly and everyone cheers as they see the coach turning into the car park. The Spanish kids are standing up in the windows waving at us. Jason kicks the ball at the bus window where Sergio is and gets told off by Mr Evans; Ana starts banging on the window to Holly; beside me, Fern is jumping up and down and waving like a lunatic to Dolores who has such a big grin on her face it looks like it's going to split in two. Soon they all start piling off the bus and hugging each other. I stand back, feeling a bit out of it, and notice Adam doing the same.

'Shame Nacho couldn't come,' I say sympathetically.

'Yeah. Never mind. I think we'll get on all right.'

'We?' The penny drops. 'Have they sent you someone else in Nacho's place?'

'Yeah,' says Adam casually. 'They rang my mum last night to ask if we'd have him. Apparently he wants to study English at uni so she could hardly say no. She's not bothered though. She said, "What's one more body in this house?"'

'Lucky!' I feel a right Billy No-Mates now. The only one without a return exchange partner. 'Who is it, Ads?'

Adam nods towards the bus. One last figure is getting off it, his backpack over his shoulder. He's not that much taller than the others, but he looks older. It's the broad shoulders and the blue-tinged jaw that does it. He looks straight at me and my heart stops.

'It's Nacho's older brother,' says Adam. 'Remember him? He's called Pablo.'

'Hi!' he says and his smile jump-starts my heart again. The problem is, it brings all the blood in my body rushing to my face too in a surge of electricity. I must look as if I've been turned upside down and stood on my head.

'Are you OK, Jaime?' asks Adam. 'You've gone a funny colour.'

Thanks, Adam, for pointing this out. So would you if the last time you were with Pablo you had your tongue rammed down his throat. Pablo is staring at me with concern, his smile fading. Say something, Jaime, quick.

'Hi.'

Is that the best I can do? It does the trick though because Pablo says uncertainly, 'This is good, yes? I see you again.'

'Good, yes,' I repeat, like I've forgotten how to speak English myself. Inadvertently my eyes move to his feet and then, guiltily, back to his face. Has he forgiven me for vomiting all over his shoes?

His smile broadens.

My blush deepens.

'Well, not good for poor old Nacho,' says Adam, a note of censure in his voice.

'No! Poor Nacho! How is he?' I start babbling but then other people recognize Pablo and ask the same question and Dolores and Ana come over to say hello and give me a hug. Then there's a mass mingling and milling about, with everyone hugging, chatting and catching up with each other, like they haven't been on Facebook every day for the past two months. The end of school bell goes and kids pour out of the gate and there's chaos, with parents turning up in cars to collect the Spanish arrivals and Señor Hairy Ears (he's back!) and Miss Martínez running around with clipboards ticking lists. Finally everyone disperses, except for the hardy few who live close to school and have to walk it. Which is pretty much Adam, Pablo and me.

'Sorry, mate,' says Adam. 'Got to walk. My mum and dad are at work.'

'No problem,' says Pablo. He hoists his backpack on to his shoulder and we fall into step together.

'How's Concha?' I ask.

He shrugs. 'The same.'

'Devil child!' says Adam and pretends to shudder.

Pablo laughs. 'She's not so bad!'

I glance at him, wondering if Concha had got her way in the end and they were going out but it's hard to tell. Pablo gives nothing away. His eyes meet mine and he smiles. I look away quickly before my cheeks start burning again.

As the days go by, things work out. The awkwardness recedes as we start to hang out together. The more time I spend with Pablo, the more I relax and stop dwelling on that last night in Spain and the less I worry about Concha. He never mentions her. Anyway, Tira whispers to me, what the hell? Concha's over there and he's over here and, let's face it, you're never ever going to see her again. The coast is clear.

But Pablo never makes a move on me, even though, increasingly, I wish he would.

It's nice having him around though. It starts to feel as if he's my exchange partner without the hassle of having him to stay. Not that it would be a hassle, but it might be a bit awkward having to negotiate bathrooms and stuff. (My personal horror!) He kips at Adam's but in school he spends most of the time with me, if he's not kicking a football around, that is. I think he finds the boys in my year a tad young. Well let's face it, they are compared to him, he should really be at the Sixth Form College; plus, personally, I think they are so immature sometimes they are bordering on infantile.

'What's it like living with Adam?' I ask him one lunchtime. I'm lying on my back on the grass and he's stretched out beside me. We've just had a particularly rubbish lesson with Holly, Adam and Jason being chucked out of class and the rest of us getting yelled at. Holly is off the wall lately. Fern says she's upset because she thinks her dad is seeing someone. Her parents are on the verge of divorce, but Holly still lives in hope they'll get back together again. Adam and Jason are always mucking about in class. Sometimes I get really fed up with it.

'It's OK. Adam is a . . . how you say . . . ?' He struggles for words.

'Nutter? Psycho? Headcase?' I suggest helpfully.

Pablo laughs. 'No. A fun guy. He likes to have fun.'

'He's a mushroom.'

'A mushroom?'

'A funghi. Get it?' Pablo turns his head and looks at me uncomprehendingly. I laugh at his puzzled expression. 'Never mind. What about you? Are you a fun guy?'

'No,' he says decisively. 'I am older. And more serious.'

Our faces are so close I can feel his breath on my

cheek. I am quiet for a moment then I say, daringly, 'I like serious.'

Pablo props himself up on one elbow and contemplates me, his heavy-lidded eyes half closed. I shade my eyes from the sun . . . and from him. I wish I hadn't said that now. I feel a bit nervous under his scrutiny. Move on, Jaime.

'What are the rest of his family like?'

He considers. 'His mother is nice. And his sister.'

Jenna? That's a surprise. Adam's younger sister is in Year 8 and to me she seems as daft as her brother. 'What's his kid brother like?'

'Like Adam only more . . . annoying.'

'More annoying than Adam? Impossible!' He smiles down at me. He is so good-looking. 'That's a big word, annoying,' I say lazily. 'Your English is improving, Señor.'

What am I doing? Flirting with him, like a nineteenth-century milkmaid.

'Thank you, Señorita.' He moves closer. 'That's because I have a good teacher. And a beautiful one.' He leans over me, blocking out the sun, and plants a kiss lightly on my lips. My heart skips a beat then my hand reaches up to the back of his head to pull him close.

The next second it nearly arrests as a football blasts into the side of my head and I spring upright in shock.

'ADAM!'

'Goal!' he yells. 'Come on, Pablo, we need you!'

Pablo jumps to his feet and dribbles the ball back to the others. 'See you later!' he calls to me over his shoulder.

Thanks, Adam. Get lost, why don't you? You are so immature.

I'm into older and serious myself.

I lock myself in my bedroom all night, thinking about Pablo, ignoring Mum when she calls up to tell me our favourite programme is on. Why would I want to watch telly with her when my own life is so much more interesting?

I know Pablo and I are going to get together soon, I just know it. The only question is, when? I just want to be with him again.

I know he feels the same. He thinks I'm beautiful!

I am so convinced he's going to ask me out I jump out of my skin every time my phone bleeps but the only texts I get are from Fern to find out if he's asked me yet and one sad one from Holly to say, 'My mum's in bits. I hate my dad.'

At last, after ten, the home phone rings, and I race downstairs to get it but Mum's already there. 'It's for me,' she says with a false smile. 'Put the kettle on, Jaime, and make us both a cuppa.' She waits until I've left the room before she starts talking into the phone. Smug cow!

The kettle's already boiled by the time she's finished yapping and made her way to the kitchen, a small self-satisfied smile on her face.

'Who was that?' I ask grumpily, splashing milk into two mugs of tea.

'Just someone from work,' she says vaguely and the annoying smile disappears as she notices the scowl on my face. She looks as if she's about to say something but then she bites her lip, opens the fridge door and pours herself a large glass of wine instead.

'Binge drinking is a real problem in middle-aged women,' I say conversationally. For a second her eyes flash in anger then she turns to leave the room.

'I thought you wanted a cup of tea!' I shout but the door slams shut behind her.

The next morning I'm up at the crack of dawn, washing and straightening my hair, pressing my shirt and putting my face on ready for school. I don't normally try so hard but today is special. I'm going out with Pablo tonight.

No actually, he didn't ring me last night, but it doesn't matter. You see, I realized in the early hours as I tossed and turned, willing him to contact me, that he didn't need to! How stupid was I? I'd forgotten that we already had a pre-booked date for tonight; Miss Martínez had arranged for the exchangees to go to the cinema together to see the latest James Bond movie.

'You are going?' Pablo had turned to me when she'd told us a few days ago. I was about to say, 'No, not my sort of film, it's a boy thing,' when I managed to stop myself just in time.

'Yeah, I think so. Are you?'

'Yes. If you are.'

'Cool.'

We were bound to sit together. And he was bound to walk me home afterwards. Let nature take its course!

'You've got to eat something!' says Mum. 'What's wrong with you?'

'Nothing's wrong with me!'

'You're looking a bit peaky!' She peers at me. 'Jaime! You can't go to school wearing all that make-up!'

'I'm just trying to look a bit healthier!'

She places her palm on my brow. 'If you're not well, you should stay off school,' she says worriedly. 'I'll get Mrs Bick in to sit with you.'

'No!' I shake her hand away crossly. 'I don't want to miss school. I'm fine.'

'Are you sure?'

'Yes!'

'Well, I'll see you at teatime. I was going to go straight out after work, but I can cancel.'

'No!' I say quickly. 'Don't do that. There's no need.'

'We'll see.' She looks unsure. 'There is a dinner ready for you in the fridge which you can . . .'

'. . . heat up for two minutes in the microwave. I know. I've had plenty of practice lately.'

She looks annoyed. 'Right then, suit yourself. I'll see you later,' and the next minute she's gone, clip-clopping crossly up the street in her high heels and tight skirt. She never used to dress like that for the office. Mind you, she never used to go straight out after work either. It's not fair. If I wasn't going to the cinema tonight, I'd be facing another evening in on my own.

It's not much fun being an only child if your single parent is permanently out gallivanting.

But what do I care? I've got a whole lovely day and, even better still, an entire wonderful evening with Pablo to look forward to!

Things never go according to plan though, do they? There's no sign of Pablo at school and Adam hasn't got a clue where he's got to.

'Dunno,' he says when I ask. 'He was still in bed when I left.'

I try to text him during registration but I get caught and my mobile is confiscated, plucked from my grasp by the evil talons of my eagle-eyed form teacher.

'You can have it back at the end of the week!' she rasps.

'That's stealing that is!' I protest but she raises one brow and silences me with her gimlet eye.

'Ask your mother to explain in writing why you need to text in schooltime and you can have it back tomorrow,' she says icily.

Yeah, like that's going to happen.

'And while we're at it, Jaime Packer, go and wash that muck off your face.' She clucks disapprovingly as I flounce past and mutters something to herself that sounds suspiciously like, 'I don't know what's got into that child lately!'

Evil, scraggy old bird!

The day goes downhill after that, mainly because first of all I keep expecting Pablo to turn up and then, when he doesn't, I worry where he's got to. I can't concentrate and don't those teachers notice! The end of the school day can't come quickly enough but then, when the bell goes, I remember that Mum's going straight out after work and, forgetting momentarily that I'm still mad at her, I feel even more fed up.

'Come home with me,' says Fern, so I do and have tea with her family. I love it in their house. We sit round the table and her dad teases her kid sister all the time, pinching her chips when she's not looking and pretending to choke to death on a fish bone. It's obvious he loves her to bits.

I wish I had a dad to pinch my chips.

Afterwards we go up to Fern's bedroom to get ready.

'Can I borrow something?' I ask. 'I don't want to go in school uniform.'

'Take your pick,' she says and flings open her wardrobe. I rummage through carefully and finally choose a striped fitted top with a little hood and a pink short skirt. Not really me, but Pablo likes me in bright colours, I remember him whistling his appreciation on Good Friday.

'This OK?'

'Help yourself.'

It's fun getting ready. I do my own make-up then help Dolores with hers. She's never worn any before because her mum's strict about stuff like that. Most of the Spanish mothers are. That's probably why Concha got away with so much because she hadn't got a mum around to keep an eye on her. Then Fern does my hair in a high ponytail which makes a change for me because I always wear it hanging down round my face.

Hiding behind it, Mum used to say. Like a pair of curtains. Yeah, well, Mrs Gadabout, I'm not hiding now!

'Look at you!' says Fern admiringly. 'You look fantastic!'

I don't look like me, that's for sure.

More like Tira.

On the way to the cinema we talk about Holly.

'She's really losing it at the moment,' I say. 'She got into trouble again today for not handing in her history homework.'

'She's upset because her mum and dad are splitting up,' says Fern.

'Poor Holly. Last night her mother crying. Ana tell me,' says Dolores haltingly. 'Holly, no time homework.'

'Apparently her dad's seeing someone else.'

'Parents, hey!' I say feelingly. Fern nods wisely, but she hasn't got a clue.

Outside the cinema there's a long queue. Holly and Ana are there already, keeping our places while Señor Hairy Ears walks up and down, doling out the tickets.

'Hope I don't have to sit next to him,' giggles Fern.

'Me neither.' I look around for Pablo but there's no sign of him. I spot Adam with Jason and Sergio further up the queue. 'Hey, Adam!' I shout. 'Where's Pablo?'

'Decided not to come. He's staying in.'

Disappointment hits me like I've walked into a door.

Holly looks at me curiously. 'You OK?'

'Yeah. Yeah, of course.' I change the subject quickly. 'Sorry about your mum and dad, Hol.'

Her expression darkens. 'Yeah, it's doing my head in. It's all my dad's fault. They'd been going through a bad patch but I thought they'd got over it. But now my mum thinks he's seeing someone.'

'That's awful.'

'Too right. Breaking up a marriage like that. It's not right. My mum's in pieces.' Her face grows fierce. 'I'll kill the bitch when I find out who it is.'

She looks as if she means it. Luckily a cheer goes up as

the queue starts shifting forward and she and Ana move up next to Adam and the others so they can get good seats. The rest of us shuffle along behind. I don't care where I sit, I've lost interest now Pablo's not here.

Why has he decided not to come tonight? Where has he been all day?

Was it something I said?

What about that kiss on the field? What about that last night in Spain?

I don't get it. I thought he liked me. A lot.

He *asked* me to come to the cinema. Didn't he?

Suddenly, as we file slowly through the doors, I feel an elbow in my ribs. Fern nods meaningfully towards a man who's just walked into the foyer and is obviously looking for someone. He checks his watch impatiently and then goes back outside and looks up and down the street.

I look back at her, puzzled. 'Who's that?' I ask.

'Holly's dad.'

'Oh my goodness, so it is! And he's waiting for someone! She'll go ballistic!'

'Don't tell her!'

As we watch, his phone rings and he holds it to his ear, talking animatedly into it for a minute. Then he snaps it shut and rams it back in his inside pocket, looking cross. The next second he's gone, striding away down the street.

'Hah! Hah! He's been stood up!' says Fern grinning.

I know what that feels like. For a fleeting second I feel a small jab of sympathy.

I couldn't tell you what the film was about. There was the usual mixture of car chases and parachuting out of planes and fuel tanks exploding and a pretty amazing sequence of leaps and tumbles through glass roofs which did get my attention, I must admit. James Bond, in the company of some gorgeous woman with her own agenda, was in hot pursuit of, or being pursued by, I'm not sure which, some extremely nasty villains, easily identifiable by their ugliness. As usual. But what the plot was about, I haven't a clue. The thing that amazes me is how Adam and Jason, who get us all into trouble in class on a daily basis because they can't concentrate for longer than a microsecond, sit there glued to the screen for the best part of two hours, following every little twist and turn of narrative, without moving a muscle. Even the Spanish kids were spellbound, though they couldn't have understood much of the dialogue.

The trouble was, I was lost in my own thoughts most of the time, which were whirling round in my head like the helicopter blades up there on the giant screen. I kept hoping Pablo might change his mind and turn up after all so for the first half hour, every time someone walked down the aisle, I'd be twisting round and peering at them to see if it was him. Then I got hissed at by the person behind me so I sank down in my seat and tried unsuccessfully to follow the film.

Outside the cinema, Holly says, 'Anyone for a burger?' then she comes to a sudden halt. In front of us, her dad is waiting by his car.

'What are you doing here?' she asks, her face falling. 'I'm not staying at your place tonight, am I?'

Poor Holly. She never knows where she is from one day to the next. Now her dad's moved out of the family home and her mum's in bits, she trundles between the two of them like a package labelled, 'NOT KNOWN AT THIS ADDRESS'. I'd hate that. You wouldn't know where you belonged. That history homework thing wasn't her fault. She'd left her book at her dad's by mistake the night before.

'No,' he says. 'I just offered to pick you up and take you home, that's all. Your mum's not feeling too good.'

'Whose fault is that?' she says tartly but climbs obediently into the back of the car. 'Come on, Ana.'

'Can I give you a lift?' her dad asks me. 'It's Jaime, isn't it?'

I glance at him curiously. I don't know him that well, I've just met him once or twice at Holly's house, but he's always seemed nice to me. Normal and dad-like, tallish, bit of a paunch, thinning on top. Boring and middle-aged like all my friends' parents and my own, come to that. Not the type to break up his marriage and go off with another woman.

Just goes to show, you never can tell.

'No thanks, I'll walk. It's not dark yet.'

'It's no trouble.' He smiles at me and opens the passenger door. I hesitate. I've got a headache fit to burst and I've had enough of this horrible day. More than anything, I just want to get home to Mum.

'I'm passing your house,' he prompts and I give in gratefully and slip in beside him, wondering how he knew where I lived.

Holly and Ana chat in the back, but I get fed up with turning around so in the end I just sit quietly and gaze through the windscreen.

'Good film?'

'All right.'

'Not a James Bond fan then?'

'Not really. Are you?'

'Yes, big time. I was going myself tonight but I was let

down at the last minute.'

Stood up, more like. Join the club. 'Really?' I say, trying to sound polite, but it comes out bored. He doesn't seem to notice though.

'How was the exchange?' he asks.

'Good.'

'You weren't that keen on going in the first place, were you? I'm glad it worked out for you.'

I glance at him in surprise. 'How do you know that?'

'Your mum said.'

Thanks, Mum. I remember now she was talking to him at the airport. Does she make a habit of discussing my concerns with every random parent she meets? I sit there, stiff with irritation, and I think he gets the message because he glances at me then lapses into silence until he turns into my road and pulls up at the kerb outside our house.

'Here you are.'

'Thanks for the lift. Bye, Hol, bye, Ana. See you tomorrow.'

'You're welcome.' Holly's dad smiles at me. It's a nice smile but I can't help noticing his teeth are a teeny bit yellow and he's wearing an anorak. I don't get it with grown-ups. Like, he's OK husband and dad material, but who on earth would choose to go out with him, especially if he's damaged goods?

Someone who's desperate, I guess.

As I get out of the car, Mum opens the front door like she's been waiting at the window, watching for me. She looks really angry.

'Where have you been?' she demands.

'The cinema.'

'You could've let me know! I've been worried sick.'

'I thought you were going straight out after work!'

'I changed my mind,' she says. 'I thought you were ill!'

'I'm fine,' I say, a bit shamefaced, and indicate the car. 'Holly's dad gave me a lift home.'

'Yes, I can see that,' she says, glancing dismissively at him. 'Thank you,' she calls and pulls me into the house. He waves, but she's closed the door even before he's had time to start the engine.

'That was a bit rude!' I stare at her in surprise. If there is one thing Mum has instilled in me over the years it's the need for good manners.

'What?'

'You could've thanked him properly.'

'I did. Anyway, you thanked him, didn't you? How much thanks does that man need?'

That man? She sounds cross with him. Oh, I get it. Just because he's got another woman, that makes him an evil person. I forgot she was sort of friendly with Holly's mum.

'I'm going to bed,' I say crossly. I don't care anyway. I've got other things on my mind. Like where do I stand with Pablo? I go upstairs without another word and put on some music.

Later on when I'm in bed reading, Mum knocks on the door with two mugs of steaming hot chocolate in her hands.

'Can I come in?' she says.

'Yeah.' I move over for her to sit on the bed. 'Thanks,' I say, taking a mug from her hand. 'What's this for?'

She gives a little grimace and sits down. 'You were right. I was rude. To Holly and her friend. I didn't even say hello to them and I know Holly's going through a difficult time.'

'Yeah, she is.' I sip the hot drink appreciatively. She's made it just the way I like it, with swirly cream and pink and white marshmallows. She cups hers in her hands and stares pensively through the rising steam at my wardrobe, lost in a world of her own.

'Is anything wrong, Mum?'

'Oh, I'm just a bit fed up, that's all . . .'

'Why?'

She sighs. 'One thing and another. Work; Concha not coming after all my preparations . . . I know it's not your fault!' she adds hastily.

I feel mean. She looks tired and fraught. 'I'm sorry I

didn't let you know where I was,' I say.

She sighs. 'All you had to do was send me a text. I've been trying your phone all night, imagining all sorts of things . . .'

'Aahh.' I feel my cheeks reddening. 'I got my phone confiscated at school.'

'Jaime!' She stares at me in concern. 'What is going on with you?'

I'd rather her give me a row than look so upset. Her brow is riddled with worry lines. Did I make those? I get angry. Defensive.

'It wasn't my fault!' I snarl. 'It's only a flipping phone, I haven't killed anyone!'

She looks shocked at my venom, like she doesn't know me any more. I don't know me any more. This isn't me, this hostile, snapping creature. What happened to shy, harmless little Jaime? It's Tira who keeps swooping to my defence every time the going gets tough, but how can I tell Mum that? She'd think I'd gone mad.

Mum bites her lip and takes a deep breath.

'How was the film anyway?' she asks warily. 'What did you see?'

I know what she's doing. Ignoring my bad behaviour. She can't do much else. I'm too big for the naughty step. But I'm glad she's taking control, reducing my rage, bringing it back from the boil. Meet her halfway, Tira.

'The new James Bond movie.'

'Was it good?' she asks. 'I wanted to see that.'

'It was OK.' I avoid her eyes in the silence that follows. 'Thanks for coming home after work by the way,' I add finally.

'That's all right,' she says, her voice warm and normal again. 'I was far more concerned about you than a silly old film.'

My head jerks up in surprise. 'Is that where you were going tonight?'

'Yes.'

'Who with?'

'A friend.'

My heart does a flip and I hear Tira's voice re-emerging. 'What friend?'

'Pardon?' Her voice is suddenly wary again, alerted by my change of tone. 'Nobody you know.'

'Who?'

'Someone from my Spanish class if you must know.'

'Oh, what a surprise!' I say sarcastically. 'Did you ring them up and cancel?'

'What?'

'Did you cancel?'

'Yes, of course I did!' Mum swallows hard and says gently, 'Jaime? What is this? What has got into you?'

'What has got into *you*!'

178

Mum looks astonished, then annoyed. She gets to her feet and picks up my mug, still half full. 'Have you finished with this?'

'Yes. I don't want it.'

She hesitates. 'Jaime? Is everything OK?'

'Yes.'

'Only ever since you came back from Spain, something's not been right. You're different.'

'*I'm* different? It's not me that's different, it's you!'

She clicks her tongue in exasperation. 'Sometimes I wish you'd never gone on that exchange in the first place.'

'Me too!' If I hadn't, none of this would've happened.

She sighs. 'I'll say goodnight then.'

'Fine.'

She flicks off the light and closes the door, none too gently, leaving me in darkness.

It's not fine. It's not fine at all.

Liar!

Liar! Liar! Pants on Fire!

I know who she was planning to go to the cinema with tonight. A friend from evening classes? That would be the non-existent Spanish evening classes she's been going to every week? I don't think so.

I have finally worked out who it is she's been seeing.

It's Holly's dad.

How could I have been so stupid, to miss what had been going on before my very eyes?

Because it hadn't going on before my very eyes, I guess. It must have started while I was in Spain. And since then they'd been careful. But not careful enough. Everyone knew he had a bit on the side.

That bit on the side was my mum.

I should have noticed. I mean, the new hairstyle; the makeover; new clothes; losing weight . . . they're all classic signs of someone having an affair. You read about it in magazines all the time.

You idiot! They were together at the airport, weren't they? You walked past them because you thought they were a couple. She'd been gossiping about me with him while I was away.

'You weren't that keen on going to Spain, were you?' he'd said.

'*I've signed up for Spanish lessons,*' she'd said.

Yeah, right. Anything to get out of the house at night. Signed up for lessons in infidelity, more like. With my mate's father.

And now she's remembered her responsibilities at last, now she's actually remembered she's got a teenage daughter to look after, she's left him standing outside the cinema like a lovesick teenager – or a wrinkly love-rat to be more precise – and expects me to be grateful! That's why he gave me a lift home, so he could see her.

She was mad about that. That's why she didn't speak to him when he dropped me off. She doesn't want me to know about their torrid little affair. She doesn't want it to come out.

I don't want it to either.

What a mess. I could strangle her.

I won't have to though. Holly will do it for me.

'*I'll kill the bitch when I find out who it is.*'

Oh no! I gasp aloud as realization hits. This is going to get all round school. Everyone will hate my mother for splitting up Holly's mum and dad!

Everyone will hate me too.

I toss and turn in my bed, trying to shake off the thoughts buzzing round my brain like angry wasps, torturing me with their stings. When the front doorbell goes, once, twice, reverberating through the darkness, at first I think I'm dreaming, and now a giant wasp is after me, angry and insistent. But then I hear Mum's bedroom door opening and her padding downstairs. 'Who can that be at this time of night?' I hear her say to herself and I jump out of bed, suddenly anxious.

Then I hesitate, my hand on the door, as my heart leaps into my throat. It's Pablo, come to explain to me why he hadn't come to the cinema. My heart soars free now with the thrill of it all but at the same time my head says, Mum is going to be so mad at me, a boy coming round this late.

But then I hear a man's deep voice and my mother's, light with surprise, answering him. Understanding hits me with the weight of a hammer, driving my hopes back down, and it's me that's angry. It's not Pablo come to see me at all. It's Holly's father, come round to seek my mother out.

Like, what is wrong with you? Can't you take no for an answer? You're dumped, man! Get over it.

Trust my mother to take up with a stalker!

I hear footsteps and the door closing and the voices continue. She's invited him in, the idiot! Now he's going to grovel his way back into her affections even though it's the middle of the night.

Suddenly I feel scared. What if he tries it on? My mother is such an innocent, she has no experience of men. He might be Holly's father but he could be a nutter for all we know. He might demand his wicked way and Mum would be no match against him. I need help but I don't have my phone to contact anyone. I don't know what to do!

It's Tira who comes to my aid. How dare he come round here in the dead of night, messing with my mum? He's still married to Holly's mother, for goodness sake! Now is the time to put an end to this mess, once and for all! A flash of temper blazes through me and sweeps me through my bedroom door to the top of the stairs.

Downstairs in the hallway, three faces stare up at me.

My mother's face, pale and concerned.

Señor Gómez's face, dark and resigned.

Concha's face, defiant but strangely apprehensive.

'¡Hola!' I say, my knees suddenly weak, and I sit down in shock on the top step of the stairs.

Concha is totally a law unto herself. I don't know why I'm surprised that she turned up out of the blue like that, unannounced, with her father in tow. Señor Gómez explains it all to us once we're sat down eating bacon sarnies rustled up out of nowhere by Mum and drinking tea. I've never seen him drink tea before, only fiercely strong black coffee, but he doesn't seem to mind, though I do notice, and so does Mum, that he heaps spoonfuls of

183

sugar into it. They're both starving.

'We could not get anything to eat on the plane,' he explains, helping himself to another sandwich. 'Only biscuits. You had to pre-order a meal. And we just turned up at the airport to get on the first flight we could. We were fortunate to get tickets.'

'It must have been expensive, leaving it to the last minute,' murmurs Mum.

Señor Gómez shrugs. 'Yes, I am afraid so. But it cannot be helped. I am pleased that Concha has decided to come to England after all so I waste no time.' He beams at us all then leans over to Mum and says in a slightly lowered voice, 'Concha can be timid, you know. At first she refused to come.'

Concha, timid? That's like saying a crocodile is kind, a hyena is humble, a lion lacks confidence.

Mind you, for her, she's being uncharacteristically silent.

Mum nods understandingly as Señor Gómez wolfs down another bacon buttie. 'Jaime is too,' she whispers back, but it's loud enough for me to hear. They must think we're both deaf. 'It's a big step going to stay with someone in a foreign country.'

'I am sorry I could not contact you by the way,' he says indistinctly. 'Concha did not appear to have your phone number.'

She had my number, I know she did. She had our house number on the information sheet and mine in her mobile. I glance at her but she avoids my eyes and concentrates on her sandwich. She didn't want me to know she was coming.

In case I objected.

'But then, out of the blue, she changes her mind. Suddenly she wants to come. So here we are! I hope it is not too much trouble for you?'

'Not at all!' says Mum who I'm starting to realize is a really accomplished liar. (*I spent the whole weekend clearing this out. Never mind the expense!*) 'We can practise our Spanish, can't we, Jaime?' Then she looks a bit worried. 'The only thing is, Señor Gómez, I'm not sure where we can put you. I'm afraid you're going to have to sleep on the sofa.'

'No, please, Señora.' Señor Gómez leaps to his feet, brushing crumbs from his suit, all of a fluster. 'Indeed no. I book myself into a hotel. I cannot possibly lay myself at your feet, abuse your hospital . . . what you say? . . . your . . .'

'Hospitality? Perhaps you would be more comfortable at a hotel.' Mum looks relieved.

'Absolutely! I have booked one already!' It's blatantly obvious he's the one who's lying now, but he's already grabbing his bag and is halfway through the door before

Mum can object. Then he turns back. 'It's Roberto, by the way.'

'Roberto,' echoes Mum. 'I'm Catherine.'

'Cat . . . e . . . rina.' He lingers over the name, stretching it out till it becomes pretty and sexy-sounding. Mum must think so too because I swear she goes a bit pink. Señor Gómez, I mean Roberto (am I supposed to call him that too?), smiles and says, 'Goodnight.' The door slams behind him. Mum looks helplessly at Concha.

'Is he going back to Spain tomorrow or staying till you go home?'

Concha shrugs her shoulders, her hands spread wide and her mouth turned down. She neither knows nor cares. Mum sighs. 'Ah well, your bed is all made up, Concha. I hope you sleep well. Jaime, show her to her room.'

I take Concha upstairs and show her the bathroom and her bedroom. She peers inside and sniffs.

'No en-suite?'

'Sorr-ee,' I say, a bit miffed, but then she adds, '*You* insisted on one,' and I remember I did and flush guiltily.

'Sorry,' I repeat, genuinely this time, and watch as she goes across to the bed and falls on to it, dropping her bag to the side. She stretches out, crosses her arms behind her head and closes her eyes as if I wasn't there.

'Why did you decide to come after all?' I ask curiously.

Her eyes open and stare at me coldly. 'Pablo's here,' she says simply. I flush even more. 'Turn the light out as you leave,' she says and turns away.

Pablo. Of course. She must have let Pablo know she was on her way.

That's why he's been avoiding me.

The next morning, Concha is eating breakfast with Mum, all showered and fresh and dressed neatly in jeans and T-shirt, by the time I emerge in my pjs, still rubbing sleep from my eyes after a very disturbed night. I look at them both and think, that used to be me chatting merrily with Mum over my cornflakes.

'Spanish people don't eat that stuff. Concha is used to cakes and coffee for breakfast,' I say sourly.

Mum looks concerned but Concha says, 'No, Mrs Packer, this is fine. I often eat cereal, remember, Jaime?' and smiles at me sweetly as if I've forgotten her chucking cornflakes all over the floor in a strop on Good Friday morning. Mum leans over to her and says confidentially in a pseudo-whisper, 'Jaime is not at her best in the morning,' and they both titter at my expense. I shake my head and scowl at them which of course plays straight into their hands, so I turn on the telly and hunch myself over a bowl of milk and cereal in front of it, refusing Mum's invitation to join them at the table where they continue their inane chatter. What is Concha playing at? She's only been here two minutes and already she's doing my head in.

When Mum leaves for work I expect Concha to turn back into her normal surly self but to my surprise she says, 'Your mother is nice,' and she sounds a bit wistful.

I remember what she'd said about hers. *My mother is beautiful and graceful and very high-powered,* and I say grumpily, 'She's all right, I suppose. She's just ordinary.'

'Ordinary is good,' says Concha firmly. 'I think she's lovely.' For a second I feel a shaft of something sharp like when you have an injection and the needle breaks the skin, but it's more shocking because I wasn't expecting it. And the substance that is coursing through my veins is just as toxic as any vaccine: it's jealousy. She's my mum, not hers.

'We're going to be late,' I say, as if it's her fault, but she grabs her bag and follows me obediently out of the house. As we walk to school she's quiet as if she's thinking. After a while she says, 'Where does Adam live?' and I know she really means, 'Where does Pablo live?' but I take her at her word and say airily, 'Not far. How's Nacho, by the way?'

'OK, I think. He's still off school. I didn't even know

Pablo had come here instead of him for a few days.'

'Then when you found out, you decided to come as well?'

Her eyes flick up at me as she recognizes my scornful tone. 'Do you have a problem with that?'

'No.' Not half. My mind runs over the events of the past few days. Pablo and me on the field, chatting and laughing together, me helping him with his English. *'I have a good teacher,'* he'd said. *'And a beautiful one.'* And then he'd kissed me.

I know something. I'm not going to give him up without a fight.

'So,' I say, like I'm making an announcement. 'Does Pablo know you're here?'

'No. It's a surprise.'

I don't believe her. Suddenly I blurt out, 'Are you two going out?'

'I guess so.' She preens a little. My heart sinks.

'Have you kissed him?'

'What do you think?'

Of course she has. Concha gets everything she wants. I've got no chance with her around. It's not fair.

'I can't believe your father brought you over, just like that,' I say bitterly. 'You can get him to do anything you want.'

Her face darkens. 'You are so wrong,' she snaps.

190

'Yes you can,' I continue. I don't like myself like this but I can't stop. Who does she think she is, turning up like that, chasing Pablo, stealing him away from me, inveigling her way into my mother's good books? I can feel Tira emerging again, taking me over. 'You've got him twisted right round your little finger, you have. What Concha wants, Concha gets. Just ask Daddy.'

'Shut up,' she barks, furious. 'You don't know what you're talking about.'

'Snap your fingers and Daddy will do anything for his precious little girl. *My boyfriend's left me, he's gone to England, Daddy,*' Tira jeers in a horrid, falsetto voice. '*Poor little me.*'

'Shut up!'

'*Get him for me, Daddy, chase after him, catch the first plane before he gets away from me . . .*'

'Shut up! Shut up! SHUT UP!' Concha's face is livid with anger. Tira vanishes in shock and I stare at Concha open-mouthed. 'You know nothing!' she growls.

'I was only joking,' I say feebly but it's too late. For a second she stands there, quivering with rage, like a cornered, angry dog, and I don't know whether she's going to hurl herself at my throat or turn tail and run, but then she gives a massive sigh and gets her anger back under control.

'Come on,' she says, eyes downcast. 'We don't want to

be late.' Her voice is low and dejected and far more powerful than when she was yelling. She's top dog now. Without another word I do as I'm told, trotting next to her obediently, my tail between my legs.

When we get to school Concha's appearance provokes a predictable reaction from both the British and the Spanish exchangees. She's greeted with open-mouthed surprise, muted mutterings, one or two tepid hellos, and then given a wide berth. I'd be so upset if no one was pleased to see me, but she doesn't seem to notice. She's only got eyes for one person. But he's nowhere to be seen.

'What's *she* doing here?' asks Fern from the corner of her mouth as Concha sweeps past her into the classroom, ignoring Dolores's startled exclamation.

'She came last night. Changed her mind.'

'Like, why?'

Fern, never subtle at the best of times, stares at her goggle-eyed as Concha surveys the classroom with her hands on her hips, oblivious to the stupefied stares from those not fortunate enough to have made her acquaintance. Satisfied that he's not here yet she shouts over, 'Jaime? Where does Pablo sit?'

I gesture towards the table at the back where a couple of girls have parked their bums to chat before school starts. Concha goes over and treats them to a full-on glare and, without a word, they get up and move to the next table. She takes their place. Fern blinks in astonishment as the penny drops.

'Is she after . . . ?'

'Pablo.'

'*Your* Pablo?' hisses Fern and I turn her away quickly in case Concha hears.

'Sshh! He's not *my* Pablo. Where is he anyway?'

'Haven't seen him. Ask Adam.'

The trouble is, Adam, as usual, is late for school, and by the time he lumbers in during registration, I'm in the middle of introducing Concha to my form teacher. To be fair, Adam looks the only person remotely pleased to see Concha and manages to give her a high five and a 'Wicked!' before he gets it in the ear from Mrs Mears for being late. There is no sign of Pablo but I have no chance of interrogating Adam because we move straight into double history after registration with old Mearsy (groan, it shouldn't be allowed!). So it's break time before the mystery is solved.

'Pablo? Gone to college,' Adam, in the canteen, crams a doughnut into his mouth.

'College? How come?' I gaze at Concha in consternation. If I'm disappointed, she looks gutted.

'He's been talking to my sister. Saying it was a waste of

time him being here, he wasn't learning anything,' says Adam, munching away contentedly on sugary fat. 'She said he should go to college with her. He's gone this morning to enrol.'

'With Jenna?' I ask, puzzled, glancing over at Adam's younger sister on the other side of the canteen with her noisy gang of Year 8 mates.

'No, stupid, with Jude.'

I'd forgotten about Adam's older sister. She was in Year 11 at our school last year. Tall, blonde and good-looking if I remember rightly.

I bet he didn't take much persuading.

'Adam's sister is nice,' he'd said. I thought he'd meant Jenna. I take a sad sip of orange juice.

'I'll go to college too,' says Concha, getting up. 'Pablo is right. You can learn nothing here.'

'Cheek!' gasps Holly, who has spent the best part of the last lesson disrupting it.

'You can't,' I say, pulling Concha back. 'You're not allowed.'

'Who says?'

'You're not old enough. You've got to be over sixteen.'

'I look sixteen!'

'No you don't.' As Concha shakes off my restraining hand and pulls herself up to her full, not very impressive height, her face pouting with disappointment, I suddenly realize underneath that mop of black hair and beetling brow she doesn't look scary any more, she looks about twelve and rather lost. 'They wouldn't let you in.'

'If they let Pablo in, they'll let me in!'

'No they won't.'

It's true. They'd let Pablo come to college for a week because he was sensible and mature and would explain to them politely why he should. Anyone could see that.

They wouldn't let Concha because she was just a stroppy kid. No matter how big a tantrum she threw. This was one time that Concha would not get her own way. And she knows it. She sits down suddenly as if all the air has gone out of her. She doesn't know what to do next.

It strikes me then that if she was still in Spain, Concha would have run off at this point. That's what she did when she couldn't cope with a situation. She ran away. But she couldn't do that now, could she? She had nowhere to run to, poor thing. Without thinking, I put out my hand to cover hers. She looks up at me, startled, and I take it away quickly.

'We'll go and see Pablo after school,' I say and she nods at me, mutely.

I'm not sure if this is a wise thing to do but we need to get things sorted out with Pablo. The thing is I'm not sure it's a straightforward contest between

Concha and me any more.

Maybe this has occurred to her too because when the bell goes, she follows me meekly to the next lesson.

After school we go round to Adam's to see Pablo. Jason and his partner Sergio come with us. I'm glad there are a few of us because I'm feeling a bit stupid to be honest. You see, there's me thinking that Pablo and me, we're . . . you know . . . a sort of . . . couple . . . and now Concha turns up and claims she's going out with him too.

I've been fooling myself. But it's not just me: Fern thought we were an item too. '*Your* Pablo,' she'd said. It had been so nice spending time with him over the past few days that all thoughts of that mad last night in Spain when I had made such an idiot of myself had receded. But Concha's being here had brought it all back, and now that she was obviously going out with him, things had become more complicated. I was afraid that Concha would make him choose between us.

Don't be silly. Of course she wouldn't. She'd make the choice for him. This is Concha we're talking about.

Either way, I had a bad feeling about it all. But I had to go because I'd promised and, to be fair, I owed it to Concha. She'd been as good as gold all day, getting on quietly while Holly, Adam and Jason fooled their way through lessons. In fact, I was a bit concerned about her, she seemed in a world of her own. But then, as we turn into Adam's street, she asks, 'What's wrong with Holly?'

'Nothing,' says Adam. 'We were just mucking about.'

'Not our fault old Smithy blew a fuse in maths,' agrees Jason.

'You were being prats,' I say. 'Adam is always a prat, Concha. So is Jason. But you're right, Holly's got issues. Her dad's left home and she's finding it hard. She's getting into more and more trouble at school every day.'

'Poor thing,' says Concha and I glance at her in surprise. Sympathy is the last thing I'd expect from her.

'Yeah, he's got a bit on the side,' explains Jason in his usual sensitive way and I can't help it, I freeze. Soon everyone's going to find out my mum is the 'bit on the side'. Beside me it's Concha's turn to look at me curiously but then the next second she comes to an abrupt halt. I follow her gaze up the street.

Coming towards us is Pablo. He's with Jude. They're walking very closely together and he doesn't notice us because he's too busy chatting and having fun.

He reaches to pull the rim of her hat down over her nose and her laugh peals out, loud and ringing. I hate girls who have the confidence to wear hats and who laugh too loudly. So does Concha apparently, the way she's looking at her. Then Pablo looks up and his eyes widen in surprise.

'Hey, Concha!' he yells. Her face clears and she runs to him. I sort of expect him to pick her up and swirl her round or enfold her in his arms and plant a huge kiss on her lips, but that doesn't happen. Instead he puts his arm round her and when she gazes up happily at him, he rumples her hair like you would a little kid and says, 'What are you doing here?' in Spanish, as if he can't think of a single reason why she would have come.

Men can be so dumb.

She answers him shyly, also in Spanish, and he laughs indulgently and gives her a squeeze.

My heart plummets into my shoes. That's it then. I might as well leave now. Concha smiles blissfully up at him, her face alight with happiness, and Adam makes sick noises. His sister flicks some screwed-up paper at him. 'Don't be mean!' she says. Jason and Sergio feast their eyes on her appreciatively.

I'd forgotten how gorgeous Jude was, with her blonde hair peeking out from under her hat and her skinny jeans and tight white T-shirt showing off all her best features. She could be a model.

I trail after them all into the house. Jenna is already home with half of Year 8; they've raided the biscuit tin and are watching TV. Jude doles out drinks and crisps and I decide she's not so bad after all. Not long after, Adam's mum arrives home from work, having picked up his little brother from school plus a couple of his friends as well. The house is full to the brim with kids in every room and soon spills over into the back yard where we discover a pair of basketball posts. Within minutes, a ball is produced and a game is organized out the back lane. I decide to hang about after all.

Pablo and Jude, in deference to their seniority, pick teams and I can't help it, I'm thrilled when Pablo chooses me first. Concha looks put out. Eat your heart out, Concepción Inmaculada! Jude chooses Jason which makes the big guy grin from ear to ear as he swaggers out to take his place beside her. Pablo picks Sergio next and I realize he is purely and simply selecting the best players for his team. So is Jude, but she's at a disadvantage because she hasn't seen most of us play. She chooses Adam, a pretty safe bet, and then they both move on to the Year 8s to get their final players. The last person to be picked is Concha who is trying . . . and failing . . . to look as if she doesn't care. By this time I'm actually feeling almost sorry for her.

The game is hilarious, with very few of the players having much regard for the rules. In fact, Jenna and her friends have hardly played it before. But what they lack in expertise, they make up for in enthusiasm, egged on by the rest of the Year 8s who make up the spectators along with Adam's little brother and his mates, who don't have a clue what's going on but like yelling, and various other kids off the estate who've come to watch.

The pace is fast and furious, with both team captains displaying a fiercely competitive streak. Adam and Jason appear to think they're playing beach volleyball as they lob the ball to each other using their fists and their wrists. The littlies don't get the dribbling bit and either hang on to the ball and run with it or pass it too quickly as if it's contaminated.

Concha objects strongly, as she, surprisingly, tries to keep to the rules, but there's no point. Even the 'professionals' are cheating. There's a lot of pushing and shoving going on and I notice Pablo, who should be above this sort of thing, using his brute strength to shoulder Adam out of his way. Mind you, Adam gets his own back by tripping him up and, in the absence of a referee, gets away with it.

Jude has got herself sorted too, having, illegally, taken up position by the basket so she can just pop the ball in whenever Jason or Adam manage to get it to her.

Obviously a netball player, our Jude. I tell Pablo and he moves over to block her, thrusting his arms up above his head so she can't receive the ball. Dirty tactics, but they work. In retaliation, Jude shoves him hard in the chest and he overbalances and falls down on to the ground, taking her with him. The two of them roll on to their backs, splitting their sides laughing, then Pablo gets to his feet and gives Jude a hand up.

The next minute, still laughing, he plants a kiss on her cheek and she (screeeech!) gives him one back full on the lips. He looks surprised then takes her face in his hands and kisses her back. Everyone cheers.

Concha, who had retrieved the ball and is waiting impatiently for play to recommence, throws it down and marches off down the lane.

'Oy! Come back! You're my best player!' yells Jude, then when Concha shows no sign of reappearing she says, 'What's up with her?'

'Bad sport,' shrugs Jason. 'She can't stand losing. Pick someone else.'

I look at Pablo but he's picked up the ball and is tapping it on the ground, waiting for the game to restart. 'I'd better go with her,' I say to him and for a second he looks a bit shamefaced but then Jude calls him and he gets on with the serious business of choosing a replacement for his team to take my place.

At the end of the lane there is no sign of Concha. I look up and down the street and make a decision to turn right, heading back through the estate towards school. Trust Concha. She only arrived in this country last night, she'd never be able to find her way back to my house on her own and my mum was going to kill me if I arrived home without her. But at the next corner I spot her ahead of me and call her name. She turns around, sees me and starts running and I curse loudly, getting told off by a passing woman for my pains, and leg it after her.

She's faster than I thought but she can't keep it up. I'm fitter than she is and eventually I catch up with her, but she still won't stop so I grab her by the arm and she stumbles to a halt. I expect her to take a swipe at me but then I see that she's crying. Her face is red, though that could be from the exertion I suppose, but her cheeks are wet and her nose is a bit runny. She sniffs hard and wipes her face on her arm.

'You OK?' I ask, though I can tell she's not. She mumbles something then fresh tears appear. I put my arm around her and lead her to a nearby wall to sit down and cry it out, wishing she could be upset a little more quietly. A bloke comes to the front door to tell us to get off his wall, takes one look at Concha sobbing her heart out and disappears back inside. People pass by but take no notice. Concha must have picked the busiest street on the estate to break her heart but I guess they're used to it round here.

Just as she gets to the hiccuping stage a woman comes along the street, turns into the house and stops to look at Concha.

'Man trouble?' she asks.

Concha nods miserably.

'Not worth it, love,' she says sympathetically, taking a not-too-clean tissue out of her pocket and pressing it into Concha's hands, before she continues on into the house. Within seconds we hear the couple inside going at it hammer and tongs. Concha scrubs her eyes with the tissue, then blows her nose in it.

'Love, hey?' she says and smiles at me weakly.

'This will make you feel better.' I place a steaming hot cup of tea in her palms and curl up next to her on the sofa with mine. Concha snorts.

'So it is true. You English think you can cure everything with a nice cup of tea,' she jeers but I notice she sips it gratefully, cradling it as if she needs the warmth.

'Not a broken heart maybe,' I say softly. She pulls a face. Daringly, I add, 'Concha? Were you really going out with Pablo?' She doesn't answer immediately but she doesn't get up and storm off either so I wait patiently. Finally she says, 'Well, I thought I was but . . . maybe I was kidding myself. Wishful thinking. He was always nice to me.'

'He was nice to me too.'

'Did you really snog him in Spain?'

I hesitate, as that mad, bad night flashes before my eyes. 'Yes,' I admit and pray that she won't ask me any more questions.

'I *knew* you had.' Her eyes flash with anger. 'That's why I came as soon as I knew he was here. I didn't want you getting your hands on him again.'

I look away guiltily. I can feel her studying me. After a while she says, 'You've got together, haven't you? Since he's been over here?'

'Yes.' It's my turn to sigh. 'I've been an idiot.'

'That makes two of us then.'

'I liked him,' I admit. 'We'd been spending a lot of time together and I sort of thought we were a couple. But he doesn't see it like that.'

'Obviously!' For a moment she sounds almost gleeful. 'He's into that long-legged *jirafa* Jude if you ask me.' But then her face crumples and she looks stricken.

'Jirafa?' Oh, I get it. Giraffe. Another new Spanish word to add to my vocabulary. 'Maybe he is at the moment. It'll be someone else next week. The guy is hot and he knows it.'

Concha looks distraught. 'I thought he was the one!' she wails. 'He kissed me you know. Loads of times.'

My heart misses a beat.

'On the lips?'

She stares at me wildly.

'Has he snogged you?' I persist, doggedly.

She bites her lips, then says, 'No.' Then she adds, almost primly, 'He wouldn't do that.'

I feel so churned up inside.

Part of me, Tira, is triumphant, gloating. I'm one up on Concha. He snogged me all right. It was me he fancied.

Part of me, Jaime, is ashamed. How easy Pablo must have thought I was, compared to all those well-brought-up Spanish girls. Even Concha. A right push-over. A piece of cake. Easy meat. Bit like tapas. Have a nibble and then try something else. Come back for more till you find something tastier on the menu.

Mind you, if he'd fancied her, he'd have snogged her too. He had plenty of opportunity.

Suddenly, I'm fed up with it all, going round and round in circles like this. I'm well brought up too. At least, I always thought I was. Now Tira is increasingly taking me over and my mother is acting completely out of character, I'm not so sure. But I know one thing: I'm sick of all this pretence.

'He's not into you, Concha. He likes you all right, but not in that way. He just thinks of you as a kid.'

Harsh but true. I wait, holding my breath, to see what effect this home-truth has on her.

'I LOVE HIM!' she howls and the tears start flowing again. I wonder whether to give her a cuddle but Concha doesn't seem to me to be the cuddly type so I nip to the loo and tear off masses of toilet paper instead. By the time I get back she's starting to get a grip.

'It's not that bad,' I say consolingly, dumping sheets of tissue into her lap. 'He's not two-timing you and he hasn't dumped you. He just hasn't noticed you in that way. Maybe one day he will. Who knows? But don't waste your life hanging round waiting. You don't need him. There are plenty more fish in the sea.'

I should've been a counsellor, me. Concha scrubs her eyes furiously, blows her nose hard, rolls up the ton of loo paper and lobs it into the bin. 'Yeah, like they're all queuing up to attach themselves to my line,' she says mournfully. 'I bet you're just clearing the decks so you can get right back in there when Jude moves on.'

'No,' I say regretfully. 'Pablo and I are history.' It's the truth. I'm seeing things clearly at last.

Concha peers at me through small, pink-rimmed eyes, still quivery, like a solitary little mole with a thick black fringe. 'Anyway,' she adds, a tad resentfully to my way of thinking, 'since when did you get to be so wise?'

I sigh heavily. 'Since my mother got to be so stupid.'

It's Concha's turn to listen to my problems. I don't know why I do this, tell her all about my mum, except that she seems different now that I've seen her crying her eyes out, softer somehow. Anyway, we're mates now, united by Pablo's casual indifference.

I tell her how it's only ever been the two of us, Mum and me, as long as I can remember but now she's got somebody else and she's not even admitting it to me, it's their little secret and I'm not part of it. Even to my own ears I sound like a whining little kid, *'nah, nah, nah, nah,'* on and on, but Concha listens intently and doesn't interrupt.

Finally, coming to the end of my tirade, I say bitterly, 'If I hadn't gone on exchange it wouldn't have got this far. They had all the time in the world to be together while I was away. Though they must have started their affair before then.'

'Affair? Is he married then?'

'Yes.'

Concha sighs heavily. 'You can't be responsible for your parents 24/7.'

I glance at her, surprised by her understanding. She gives me a rueful, comforting little smile. 'Who is it then?'

'That's the trouble,' I groan. 'It's Holly's dad.'

'NO!' She stares at me open-mouthed, her eyes wide with astonishment. 'Poor Holly!'

Poor me! 'I wish I hadn't told you now!' I'm surprised by the vehemence of her reaction, to be honest. If bad girl Concha is as shocked as this, what is everyone else going to say? 'Nobody else knows,' I warn her fiercely. 'Not Holly, not anyone.'

'I won't say a thing!' she says hastily. There's the sound of a key in the lock and we turn round guiltily to watch Mum letting herself in through the front door. She smiles brightly at us.

'*¡Hola!*' she says cheerfully. 'Sorry I'm late. Are you both famished?'

'Where have you been?' I ask coldly.

'Shopping.' She holds her bags aloft. 'I stopped off at the supermarket on the way home from work. I thought I'd try a paella tonight in honour of Concha. OK?'

'Whatever.' I turn away from her.

'Do you like paella, Concha?' Mum asks anxiously. 'I can do something else if you prefer.'

'Paella would be lovely, thank you, Mrs Packer,' says Concha, smiling politely at her, like she's just graduated from charm school.

'Your father can join us if he likes,' says Mum, beaming at her with relief. 'Give him a ring.'

'Not out tonight then?' I challenge.

'No.'

'No Spanish lessons? No James Bond movie? No hot date?'

'Hot date?' Mum's eyes narrow and she looks at me

strangely. 'What are you talking about, Jaime?'

'Nothing. Anyway, it's nice to have you home for a change,' I say sarkily. 'Come on, Concha, let's go upstairs.'

I can feel Mum's eyes boring into me as Concha follows me up the stairs and into my bedroom. Inside, I slam the door and fling myself on to my bed.

'See! See what she's like? She just makes out all the time that there's nothing going on. It's doing my head in.'

Concha sits down on the floor, her back against my bed, and takes out her phone, tapping it against her chin pensively. 'She seemed a bit surprised to me.'

'Of course she was surprised! She didn't know I'd rumbled their little game. Only it's not a game, is it? It's serious.' I roll over and raise myself up on to my elbows, my face in my hands, and groan out loud. 'The cow! How could she break up a marriage like that?'

'Maybe it was over before she got together with him.'

'So? It's still Holly's dad. She knew how gutted Holly was when her dad left. She knows her mum, for goodness sake.'

'Does she? That sucks.'

'I know. Holly's going to hate me.'

'It's not your fault,' says Concha comfortingly. 'Perhaps she'll dump him.'

'Huh! Goodness knows what she sees in him in the first place. His teeth are yellow and he wears an anorak!'

'Gross!' Concha visibly shudders. 'Parents, hey? They should know better at their age. Why can't they learn to behave themselves?'

Coming from Concha who smokes, drinks, picks fights with everyone, is boy-crazy, rides round on scooters all night and gets chucked out of schools, that's rich. She's staring at me with such an indignant, self-righteous expression on her face, I can't help it, I start giggling. She looks surprised.

'What?'

'You! Listen to yourself!'

For a second she looks annoyed then she sees the funny side. She grabs my pillow off the bed and chucks it at me. I grab the other one and smack her over the head with it, the whole force of my weight behind it. Soon we are having a full-on pillow fight and we don't even notice Mum standing at the doorway watching us until one of the pillows bursts and feathers start floating down all over the room.

'Don't you think that's enough?' she says coldly, her arms folded. 'Now get this cleared up.'

'Sorry, Mrs Packer,' says Concha meekly and she does as she's told, scooping up armfuls of feathers and dropping them in the bin. I start sneezing immediately and stand there watching her, convulsively exploding, until Mum barks, 'Give her a hand then!'

and I jump to it, sneezes or not.

'You used to be such a good girl,' she remarks, shaking her head in disapproval. I feel like I'm about six again and she's caught me drawing on my bedroom wall.

'So did you!' I mutter.

'What?' She looks at me suspiciously then she turns to Concha. 'Have you rung your father yet? Because dinner won't be long.'

'Sorry, Mrs Packer,' repeats Concha and picks up her phone off the floor. 'I'll do it now.'

The door closes behind Mum. '*Sorry, Mrs Packer,*' I echo in a silly high voice. 'Why are you so nice to her?' I add grumpily, picking up feathers as Concha presses buttons and puts the phone to her ear. They're everywhere. It'll take ages to clear them all up and I'll be sneezing all night.

'Because she's nice. Why are you so nice to my dad?'

'Because *he's* nice.'

'No he's not. He's horrible. Hi, Dad!' Her face lights up as he answers. 'Can you come over to Jaime's for dinner? Now! What? Well come as fast as you can.'

She snaps her phone shut. 'He said he's coming but he might be a bit late.'

'Why?'

'He didn't say. I bet he doesn't come anyway.'

'Why not?'

Her eyebrows rise. 'Duh! He doesn't want to spend time with us, stupid. He's got other fish to fry.'

'Like?' She's lost me now.

'Like your Miss Martínez. He fancies her.'

'Does he?' I don't know why I'm surprised. Everyone does. Come to think of it, I'm sure I remember him ogling her in Spain. Ugh! He's too old for all that. And he's a dad!

Doesn't make any difference though, does it? Look at my mum and the way she's been acting.

'You bet he does. I reckon that's the only reason he agreed to bring me here in the first place.'

Señor Gómez does come, even though he's late. He's clutching flowers and wine and reeking of aftershave.

'I must apologize for my delay, Caterina,' he says, doing his clicky heel thing as he presents his offerings to Mum.

'Not at all,' she says graciously, even though for the past hour she's been pacing the floor muttering to herself about food spoiling and poking the paella round. She accepts them as if they're the finest bouquet and vintage she has ever received instead of a bunch of supermarket flowers with the price still on, guaranteed for seven days, and a wine on special. It strikes me what impeccable manners they both have. I feel a flush of pride in my mum before I remember she's been cheating on her friend and I don't like her any more.

'I have been meeting with your teacher, Señora Martínez,' he says as we sit down at the table. The bread roll I've just taken a bite out of gets stuck in my throat and I find myself choking. Concha helpfully bangs me on the back. 'Didn't waste much time then!' she mutters under her breath as Señor Gómez turns to look at Mum, who comes in from the kitchen bearing a mountain of paella wafting delicious odours. Señor Gómez inspects it appreciatively as she places it on the table before him.

'I've never made it before,' she says anxiously. 'I hope it's all right.'

'*¡Muy delicioso!*' he pronounces, inhaling with approval. 'Chicken, chorizo, shrimp, mussels, squid . . . you have done us proud, *Señora*.'

Mum goes pink with pleasure and pushes the dish of rice and fishy things towards him. Señor Gómez talks non-stop as he ladles it on to his plate. 'I take longer than I think with Señora Martínez . . .' Concha and I exchange a look. 'There are many forms to sign, for insurance and other purposes . . .' He drones on and I switch off as Mum rescues what's left of the paella and passes it on to Concha and me. We serve ourselves and get stuck in. He's right. It is *'delicioso'*. How come my mum can produce something like this? She's full of surprises. '. . . and all because Concha does not travel with the others,' he finally concludes and starts to eat his food.

'Will she be going back with them?' asks Mum.

'Unfortunately, no,' says Señor Gómez indistinctly as he spears a particularly tasty king prawn and chews and swallows it rapidly. 'It is not possible. She has no ticket. So I must stay until they return to Spain next week and escort her home myself.'

'Poor you,' mutters Concha sarcastically, but it's wasted on her father who leans over courteously to top up Mum's wineglass. He's looking remarkably cheerful, no doubt because he's busy working out in his head how many nights he has left to seduce the gorgeous Maria Martínez.

After dessert, shop-bought profiteroles (thanks, Mum, no need to keep apologizing to Señor Gómez, it's obvious he's enjoying them as much as we are), Concha and I disappear back upstairs while Mum makes liqueur coffees for herself and our guest. I bet he thinks we dine like this every night!

'Great dinner,' says Concha, throwing herself on my bed and groaning. 'I'm so full.'

'Budge up.' I lie down beside her and flick on the bedside lamp to create a soft pool of yellow light that laps gently at the dark corners of the room. 'Remember the meal I had at your place on my first night? It was amazing.'

'Tapas. Abuela spent all day making those for you.'

'She made me some to take home as well.' I lie there

in the semi-darkness thinking of Abuela, with her papery, powdery skin, criss-crossed with fine lines, her smell of lavender, and her hairy kisses. 'I loved Abuela.'

'I know. She adored you too. *Why you not like the little English girl?*' Concha does a fair representation of Abuela in screeching mode and I laugh. Then she adds softly, 'I was soooo jealous of you that day on the beach.'

'Why?' I ask, genuinely surprised. I lever myself up on to my elbows and look down at her. She looks young and defenceless, lying there on her back. I wonder how I ever found her scary?

'You got on so well, chatting away together. It was like she was your grandmother, not mine.'

'I wish she was,' I say quietly. Then I add, 'She loves you too.'

Concha snorts. 'I don't think so!'

'Don't be daft!'

'The poor old bag has to come and look after me every time my dad goes away on business. She probably hates it.'

'Of course she doesn't!'

'I'm a nightmare,' she says matter-of-factly. 'Why would anyone love me?'

'*She does!*' I insist, surprised she doesn't believe this. I remember Abuela stroking her brow as she slept, smoothing her hair, praying over her. And Concha knows this too; she was awake at the time. 'She was always fussing over you, making sure that you were OK.'

'That's only because she feels sorry for me.' Concha's voice is grumpy. She turns away from me and buries her face in the pillow, her back a hunched barrier between us.

'Why?' I'm genuinely puzzled. 'Why would she feel sorry for you?'

'Because,' she says, her voice muffled, but still clear enough to hear, 'my mother left me. Twice.'

Concha tells me the whole story, lying on my bed with her arms behind her head, staring at the ceiling. Her mum and dad split up when she was ten.

'Life was all right when I was a kid,' she says simply, 'until I got into double figures. Then it went all wrong.

'I don't really know what happened,' she continues. 'My mother was beautiful . . . is beautiful . . . and clever and successful. Like my father, she ran her own company. She was often away on business trips, all over the world: France, Italy, the States, the UK, everywhere. Abuela would come and look after me when she was away. When I was older, my mother said, she would take me with her. But one day she went to work in America and she didn't come back.'

Her face darkens. 'My father said she was busy, she

would be home soon. I believed him. Time went on and whenever I got anxious, always he would say, 'Your mother would not abandon you, sweetheart.' Then one day I overheard him talking to Abuela. He told her they were getting a divorce and she should come to live with us permanently to care for me. Abuela was angry with him. I don't think she wanted to look after me.'

'Maybe she was angry because he was divorcing your mother.'

Concha shrugs. 'Maybe. I was angry too. He had lied to me. I wanted my mother. I did not want to stay with my father who told lies or my grandmother who did not want to look after me. One day we went to court and I told the judge I wanted to go to America to live with my mother.'

She looks as if she's about to cry. I can't help noticing her Spanish accent has thickened as she becomes more emotional.

'I lived with her for nearly three years. It was not easy. My mother likes her own way . . .' She gives me a sideways look and a little crooked half-smile. 'I know, don't tell me, that's who I get it from. When she was there we clashed a lot. But most of the time I was left with housekeepers while she went about her business.

'It was cold. I missed my father and my grandmother. I had no one to talk to. At school I was the weird kid who came and went by taxi and couldn't speak English properly. By the time I'd learned how to, I hated those kids who'd left me out of their games. I didn't want to be friends with them any more.'

I picture fierce little Concha, standing alone in the playground, pretending she didn't care, grimly protecting her pride. Then, after school, home in a taxi to a solitary tea, served by a succession of anonymous housekeepers.

What a lonely existence.

'Is that why you came back?'

'No.' She takes a deep breath and sighs deeply. 'It was not all work and no play with my mother. She was seeing someone. Eventually, she decided to get married again. So you see, my mother left me, not once, but twice.'

'But . . . ? Why didn't you stay with her? Didn't you like her new husband?'

She frowns like this question is irrelevant. 'He is American. He has children of his own. Plus . . .' her jaw juts out as she adds quietly, '. . . they have a baby daughter together. She has a new family now.'

I stare at her in surprise. 'You have a baby sister?'

'Yes.'

'What's her name? How old is she? What's she like?'

'Her name is Sofia, she's five months old and I've never seen her.'

'Not even a photograph?'

'My mother sends them to me but I delete them.'

'Without looking?'

'Of course.'

I don't believe her. Not for a minute.

'Has she got black hair like you?'

'A bit fairer . . .' Her eyes flash as she realizes I've tricked her and she adds quickly, '. . . so they say.'

'If I had a kid sister I'd want to see her.'

'Good for you!' Her voice is bitter. 'I'll remind you of that when your mother marries Holly's father.'

'No way! They're not going to get married!'

'How do you know?'

There's no answer to that. 'Even if they did . . .' my voice quivers, 'my mum's far too old to have another baby.'

'Are you sure about that?'

'Yes!'

But I'm not sure. What do I know? It's all got too complicated.

Me/Concha; Concha/Pablo; Pablo/me; Pablo/Jude; Señor Gómez/Miss Martínez; my mum/Holly's dad; marriage/remarriage; new families/new babies . . .

I'm not sure about anything any more.

The time flies by quickly. On the whole I've enjoyed having Concha here. Now she's opened up a bit (a lot!) and we're getting to know each other better, I like her more and more. She still has her moments and then we fight like cat and dog, but it's usually over as quickly as it started and we're back to having a laugh together. I find I can speak to her more honestly and openly than anyone else I know, even Fern. Maybe it's because I know I'll never see her again after this week is over.

At school we decide to have a farewell party at Lucky Strikes, the local ten-pin bowling alley, on the last night the Spanish kids are with us. Miss Martínez and Señor Hairy Ears (he'll always be that to me) are in charge but they leave most of the organization to us. We sit around one lunchtime planning the party while the Spanish kids are having a meeting about going back.

'Let's invite the host families as well!' suggests Holly.

'Ana's stayed at my mum's and my dad's with me, so I'll invite them both!'

My heart sinks. 'Is that a good idea?' It's obvious where she's coming from. She sees it as the perfect opportunity to get her mum and dad back together again. Fat chance of that with my mum around! I really need to keep her and Holly's dad apart. I think it might all be back on again between them. Since the paella fest for Concha and her father, my mum's forgotten the dutiful hostess act. Some nights she's gone out and left us to our own devices.

'Definitely!' says Fern. 'The Spanish kids love our parents because they give them so much freedom. Our parents love them too. My family reckon they're going to adopt Dolores.'

Funny, I don't feel jealous when I hear Fern say this. Things have changed. Now I'm just intent on keeping Unlikely Sex Goddess as far away as possible from Anorak Man.

'I don't want Ana to go home!' wails Holly. 'She keeps me sane.'

'I don't want Sergio to go home either,' wails Jason in a pretty good imitation of her voice. 'He keeps me insane!' and everyone laughs.

'Well, this may surprise you all, but I'm going to miss Concha,' I announce.

'Are you?' Fern stares at me round-eyed. 'Crazy Concha!'

'She's not crazy,' I say. 'Just a bit mixed-up, that's all.'

'Concha's OK,' agrees Adam.

'Actually, I think Concha's all right when you get to know her,' says Holly magnanimously. 'Now she's not so prickly.'

'What about Pablo?' asks Fern.

'What about Pablo?' I say shortly. 'I haven't seen him all week.'

'Not since our Jude's got her clutches into him,' says Adam cheerfully. 'They're joined at the hip.'

I can't help it, I feel a sharp twang of pain when he says that. Fern notices, of course.

'Don't forget to tell him about the party, Ads,' she says casually. Too casually.

'He knows already. He's coming.'

My heart leaps into my mouth.

'With Jude,' he continues.

It plummets straight back down to its normal place again. In my boots.

'Maybe it should be invitation only,' suggests Fern, nudging me meaningfully in the ribs. 'We could send them out by post.'

'Good idea!' Then my brain shifts away from Pablo problems and back to Mum problems and I realize, too late, I do not want an invitation landing on the mat for my mum. So I say, as casually as I can, 'Leave my mum off the list though. She won't want to come.'

'Why not? Have you asked her?' Fern looks at me curiously.

'Not yet.' Not ever, if I can help it. 'I just know she won't. She's very busy at the moment, she's out all the time . . .'

'Has she got a fella?' asks Holly eagerly. 'That's how it started with my dad, always out, never knew where he was, who he was with . . .'

'NO! Absolutely not! She's just busy, that's all. Work and that . . .'

'It'll make a nice change for her then to come to a party. I'll send her an invitation anyway.' Fern produces a little notebook and starts writing names in it officiously. She thinks she's practising for *The Apprentice* ever since she organized her mum's surprise fortieth birthday party.

'No!' I say emphatically. The last thing I want is for her and Holly's dad to go public at a school bash. Especially if Holly's mum is there too! 'Think about it, Fern. There's not enough time left and it'll cost too much to send them by snail-mail.'

She sniffs with disappointment then rallies. 'OK, I'll send them by email instead.'

Jason hoots. 'You're joking. My mum doesn't do email!'

'Nor mine!' says Adam.

'We'll just ask them, Fern,' I say soothingly. 'It'll be all right.'

'We need to know numbers!' she frets.

'No we don't,' says Adam. 'Not exact numbers. We went to Lucky Strikes for the football club Christmas party. We just hired so many lanes. So long as they've got a rough idea how many people want to eat, they don't care too much.'

'But that's if you want burgers and chips and stuff,' Fern protests. 'If we want something different . . .'

'We like burgers and chips and stuff!' says Adam, and when Fern objects, all the boys shout out 'BURGERS! BURGERS! BURGERS!' like the big kids they are, and it all descends, predictably, into chaos.

So Holly, Fern and I decide to form a committee to organize it properly and we ask our Spanish partners to join us. Then Concha says, 'Why don't we have some boys on the committee as well?' and all the others roll their eyes. Poor Concha. I think the real reason she's boy-mad is because girls don't like her, except me of course! On the other hand, it could be a ploy to co-opt Pablo, whom I know she hasn't completely given up on yet. It doesn't work though, Adam is the only one who turns up for our meeting with Miss Martínez and Señor Hairy Ears.

'You're inviting the parents?' asks Miss Martínez.

'Yes.'

'Good idea. Don't forget to ask your father, Concha.'

Concha scowls. Poor thing. Watching your parent all over your teacher is not a recipe for a good night out.

'We'll book all the lanes,' Adam says, getting stuck right in.

'Four,' amends Miss Martínez.

'Four lanes, four hours?' he asks, ever hopeful.

'Four lanes, two hours,' she says firmly.

'We don't want to spend all night bowling,' says Fern, who's appointed herself our secretary and is taking down minutes of the meeting. What is she like?

'No, you're right!' Adam's eyes gleam. 'They've got a shooting gallery. We can book that as well!'

'NO!' Fern, Dolores, Ana and I protest in unison.

'YES!' shout Holly and Concha, neither of whom, personally, I would trust within a mile of a gun.

Miss Martínez must think the same because she eyes them uneasily and suggests, 'Let's hire a room instead and have our own disco.'

'Definitely!' Fern writes down DISCO in capital letters with stars around them.

'With its own bar?' asks Adam hopefully.

'Absolutely,' says Miss Martínez. His face is comic with surprise. 'Selling Coke and orange squash,' she adds and we all laugh as Adam's face falls.

'They've got a great games room there,' says Fern, busy scribbling everything down. 'They've got a pool table and arcade games . . .'

'. . . table football and video games,' says Adam, cheering up again.

'Giant draughts, crazy golf, loads of other stuff as well. There will be stacks to do.'

'Don't forget we've got to eat,' says Adam. 'We need to book a meal too.'

Concha and I look at each other. 'Ah now, we've had an idea for that,' she says, shyly for her, so everyone looks up in surprise. Then when she starts outlining our suggestion, they all start nodding and saying, 'Brilliant!' and Fern's pen is practically flying off the page as she tries to get everything down. Our idea's gone down well with everyone it seems.

Everyone except Adam that is. 'The boys are NOT going to like that,' he states categorically.

Fern rolls her eyes. 'All those in favour of Concha's idea, put your hands up!' Everyone's hand shoots up except for Adam's. 'You're outvoted,' says Fern crisply, then, 'Great idea, Conch,' and all the girls echo, 'Yeah, great idea!' and Señor Hairy Ears pats her on the back.

Concha goes pink with pleasure, so unused is she to being praised, just like I used to. It's so nice to see I let it pass that ACTUALLY, it was my idea in the first place.

Now all we have to do is:

1. make sure my mother keeps well away from Lucky Strikes on Friday night and,

2. ring Abuela.

It's no good. She's found out. I knew she would! She comes home one evening and I can tell she's in a mood right away, even though she's trying not to show it too much in front of Concha. But I haven't lived with her for fourteen years not to recognize the signals: ramrod back; pursed lips; the way she bangs her bag down upon the worktop and starts emptying out her shopping very crossly indeed as if it's the tin of beans, frozen ovenchips and half a dozen free-range eggs that have upset her, not me.

'You'll break those eggs if you're not careful,' I point out helpfully, then wish I'd kept my mouth shut as her eyes bore into mine.

'Why didn't you tell me about the party?' she asks, cutting straight to the quick.

'I did!'

'You didn't tell me *I* was invited!'

'Didn't I?' I look wildly at Concha for help but she's frozen to the spot.

'You know you didn't!'

'I didn't think you'd want to come.'

'You didn't want me to come, you mean!' She picks the eggs out of the carton, one by one, and jabs them angrily into the fridge door.

There's silence. 'Come if you want to,' I shrug. 'It makes no odds to me.'

'Holly *wants* her parents to come. Her mother *and* her father. And you? You never even bothered to invite me. Damn!' An egg slips through her fingers and falls splat on the floor, and before I can help it, I say, 'See! I told you so!' because I knew it! I knew Holly's dad would tell her. She glares at me like it's my fault she's so clumsy then she grabs a cloth and bends down to clear up the mess. I watch as she swirls the cloth round blindly, making it worse.

Then she stops, like that, all of a sudden. She just squats there, on her haunches, doing nothing, just staring at the smeary mess on the floor with me staring at the top of her head where her roots are beginning to show. I don't know what all the fuss is about, it's just an egg, that's all, she's got another five where that came from. But as I bend down to pick up the bits of broken shell she grabs my hand and looks me straight in the eye. 'Are you ashamed of me?' she asks and her brown eyes are sad.

'No!' I snatch my hand away in shock. It's true. I'm not ashamed of her. I think she's ace. But I can't handle this, her breaking up Holly's parents' marriage, it's asking too much. I'm ashamed of what she's doing, that's the trouble, and that shame has become an ugly, awkward chasm between us, full of guilt and lies, that I don't know how to cross.

'It's our fault, we just forgot.' Concha's voice is low and soothing, bringing us both to our senses. 'We've been so busy organizing the party we forgot to invite the most important person. Please will you come, Mrs Packer?'

What is she doing? I don't want Mum there, not with Holly's dad being there as well!

'We would like you to. Wouldn't we, Jaime?' insists Concha.

'Yeah, of course,' I echo blankly.

Mum picks up the shell and gets slowly and heavily to her feet. 'We'll see,' she says, putting the bits in the bin. Then she turns and gives us a wry, watery little smile. 'It's nice to be asked anyway.'

That really shook me that did, that episode with Mum. She's not one for histrionics normally. Neither am I, come to that. We have tea – egg, chips and beans, needless to say – and then the three of us spend the night watching telly. I go to bed early and to my surprise I fall straight to sleep. All this emotion is exhausting. In the morning I feel loads better, though I still haven't solved the problem of Mum and Holly's dad.

'Don't worry,' says Concha on the way to school. 'I've got a plan.'

She's a genius, that girl! She comes up with a plot that is so simple it's brilliant. After school we arrange to meet up with Señor Gómez for coffee and he treats us to the most amazing triple chocolate fudge cake you have ever tasted in your life.

'Tomorrow night we're organizing the farewell party,' she tells him, forking chocolate goo into her mouth. 'It's going to be great. We've got a heavy rock band playing called the Rottweilers. They don't sing, they bark like dogs, and they are so loud they'll blow the roof off. Everyone will go ballistic. You're invited.'

'Ah!' he says and concentrates on his fudge cake.

'You can give us a hand if you like,' she carries on. 'Only we'll need some help keeping the boys in order. Apparently, Jaime says, at the Christmas do, all they did was get drunk and pick fights with each other.'

'Yeah, it got a bit nasty,' I lie, doing my bit. 'Some of them ended up in Accident and Emergency.'

'Dear me!' He looks alarmed.

'The parents stayed up all night clearing up the mess,' says Concha chattily.

'Sick and that,' I explain, then I add, 'vomit,' for good measure in case he doesn't understand. 'That's why we need a lot of parents there to keep an eye on things.'

He puts his fork down as if he's lost his appetite and sips his latte thoughtfully instead.

'Yeah, it's going to be brilliant! You must come!' I urge. 'In case it gets out of hand, you know . . .'

'Well . . .' He's busy searching round for an excuse when Concha hands him one on a plate.

'The only thing is . . . if you don't mind me saying, Dad . . .'

'Yes?' He looks at her hopefully.

'Maybe you should offer to take Jaime's mum out for dinner instead. Being as she's put me up for the past week or two.'

'Of course!' He looks positively transformed at the prospect.

'Only I know you'd like to join us at the party but I think it would be a nice thing to do . . .'

'Absolutely!'

'And don't take no for an answer!' I say anxiously. 'If she says she'd rather come to the party don't listen to her.'

'Don't worry,' he says, smiling at us. He can't believe his luck, being granted a get-out clause like that! 'I think

I can manage to persuade her. I will give her a ring now.'
He disappears outside to get a signal.

'Fingers crossed,' says Concha. 'If they buy that idea,
we get two for the price of one. *He* stays away from Miss
Martínez and *she* stays away from Holly's dad, plus we get
to have a good time without them around.'

She grins at me triumphantly.

'What? With the Rottweilers and all those
vomiting boys?'

She laughs out loud. Then she says, 'There's
always Pablo!'

'Concha!' My jaw drops open. 'I thought we'd agreed
he was off limits!'

'Just joking!' she laughs again. But I don't believe her.

Lucky Strikes turns out to be a great venue. The party room is cosmic! There's a big disco ball in the middle of the ceiling which circles the room, beaming luminescent lights over everyone, and dance music is belting out of the speakers. No scary Rottweiler band this, just Jason's cool older brother, Craig, who's been roped in to act as DJ for the night, armed with our latest play-list, plus some old party favourites thrown in for good measure. Round the edge of the room, tables are set ready for us to eat later, and in the corner there's a bar. Even though it serves only Cokes and juices, boys have started to huddle around it, nursing their drinks. A crowd is gathering to watch Adam and Sergio, brilliant dancers as they are, on the floor practising their hip-hop dance moves.

Next door is the games room, with pool tables and table football, arcade and video games, and loads of massive boards set out on the floor where you have to be the playing piece that jumps from square to square. Kids who wouldn't normally be seen dead playing a board game are queuing up to play draughts and snakes and ladders. Miss Martínez, in a very tight T-shirt, is playing croquet with Jason's dad while Jason's mum stands stiff as a mallet with a fixed smile on her face, trying to make out she's not in the least bit bothered. Next to them, Señor Hairy Ears is leaping up and down a giant keyboard, playing '*¡Viva España!*' with a crowd of admiring spectators egging him on.

'It's going really well!' says an eager voice at my shoulder. Fern and her sidekick Dolores seem to have assumed overall responsibility for making sure everyone is here. Fern, unbelievably, is holding a clipboard.

'Any sign of Pablo?' asks Concha, scanning the room.

Fern consults her clipboard. She has a list of names, some of which have been ticked. 'Yes, he's here,' she says. 'He must be bowling.'

Concha is off like a shot.

Dolores grins. 'She is still keen, yes?'

I nod. 'Looks like. But she's got no chance with Jude around.'

'Maybe when they go back to Spain they'll get it together,' says Fern without thinking. Then she sees my face and groans, 'Sorry!'

Dolores shakes her head. 'Pablo is a good boy. But he is . . . what do you say . . . ? He is a *coquetear* . . . a . . .'

'A flirt.'

'How did you know that?' Fern asks me admiringly.

'A coquette is an old-fashioned name for a flirt.'

'In a nice way, of course,' Dolores continues. 'He likes girls. He likes them all.'

She's right, he does. He likes Concha. He likes Jude. And he likes me. All of us. I feel a hot wave of embarrassment wash over me as I remember how I thought I was special, how I threw myself at him.

How Tira threw herself at him, I should say. Not Jaime. I wouldn't do that. Not now. Not any more.

Not now I've realized that for Pablo one girl will never be enough.

'Is my dad here?' Holly appears in front of us. 'Only I haven't seen him yet and my mum's here already . . .'

Fern inspects her list. 'I haven't ticked him in yet,' she says. I spot Holly's mum standing a little way back with Ana. She smiles at me and raises her hand in a little wave. I wave back then I find myself sighing out loud.

'What's up?' asks Holly.

'Nothing.'

How can I tell her I'm feeling sorry for myself because my mum's not here when I'm the one who's put her off coming? I can't help it though; everyone else's mum is here except mine.

'Here he is!' Holly squeals as her dad appears at the door. 'Dad? Dad! Over here!' He makes his way towards us, shouldering his way through the crowd. Who invited all these people?

'Hello, girls. Have I missed the bowling?'

'No. Come on, I need you in my team. Mum?' She darts over to her mother and grabs her by the hand. 'I need you as well.'

Holly's right. You need your parents in your team. I wish my mum had never started this thing with Holly's dad. Then we could be a team too.

'Good luck!' I call after them. Holly turns back and grins. She knows what I mean.

'You coming?' she invites.

Fern shakes her head. 'We need to check people in,' she says virtuously. Dolores looks disappointed.

Holly comes back and snatches the clipboard from Fern's hands and puts it down on the table beside her. 'Come on!' she orders us. 'We need you lot to make up the team.'

It's really busy in the bowling alley, all the lanes are in use. 'I knew we should have booked more lanes,' grumbles Adam, who's abandoned the dance floor and is waiting to play. He's organized a family team with Pablo, Jude, his mum and dad, his kid brother and sister and now Concha to make up the numbers. Pablo gives me a hug when he sees me; Concha gives me a frown. Jude doesn't turn a hair. Instead she says, 'Here! They've finished. You lot play against us!' She's so bossy!

'Who've we got?' I start counting. 'Holly, her mum and dad, Ana, Fern, Dolores, me . . . we need one more.'

'Will I do?' asks Miss Martínez, appearing at my elbow. Pablo's eyes widen appreciatively. Dolores is so right. This guy *loves* women. Concha glowers at her.

Adam runs through the rules for everyone's benefit and then the game gets underway. He's a real expert and Jude knows what she's doing too. In fact, his whole family are pretty good – it's obvious they've played before – and Pablo plays well too. (Naturally!) Very soon it's clear they're going to wipe us out.

On our team, Miss Martínez and Holly and her dad aren't bad, but the rest of us, including me, are rubbish. How hard can it be to chuck a ball in a straight line? Mine keeps going down into the gutter thing at the side. At first it's funny, then it becomes embarrassing. In the end, Adam takes pity on us and decides to use me to demonstrate a bit of technique.

'Right then. Pick up the ball.'

'It's heavy!'

'Use both hands! Now, take three paces from the Foul Line.'

'What's the Foul Line?'

'That black line there, you keep stepping over. This way, idiot!'

Everyone laughs as I take a step towards the pins.

'Idiot yourself! You're confusing me!'

'Right. Turn around and face the skittles. Stand still. Bring the ball up to your chin. Good. Now push it away from yourself in a big wide arc. Don't let go yet! Move forward, let the ball swing back. Now let go . . .'

The ball rolls smoothly away from me, down, down, down the alley, straight through the middle of the pins. Four, five, six, seven, eight skittles flash up on the screen overhead! Everyone cheers wildly, even the opposition. I shriek and jump as high as I can, punching the air, then I pick up my second ball and finish off the remaining two.

'*Tira! Tira! Tira!*' yells Concha. Everyone in the bowling alley looks at us in surprise and we burst out laughing. It's a great moment. Then it's Holly's mum's turn and she's obviously been paying attention because she tries out the same move and knocks down six pins. Holly's dad roars his approval and she looks pleased with herself.

'That was amazing!' says Fern when the game is finally

over. 'OK, they won but at least we weren't slaughtered. Hey, Jaime, you should be really proud of yourself.'

'I know! I know! I LOVE bowling!'

'I don't mean that,' she laughs and gives me a hug. 'I meant all that attention and you didn't go red. Not once. Not when Adam told you off, nor when we all cheered you.'

'I didn't, did I?' I grin at her in delight.

'I need a drink after that,' says Holly's dad. 'What can I get you, Babs?'

'Don't be too long,' says Holly. 'There's food in the next room.' She beams as we watch her father escorting her mother to the bar. Her mum perches beside him on a high stool and he leans in to listen to her above the noise of the crowd, as he fishes for money in his pocket.

They look right together. They look like a couple.

I turn away. 'Come on, you lot. It's time to eat.'

While we've all been bowling, the restaurant had done us proud. I reckon the chef was so pleased to be cooking something other than the usual burgers and chips that he'd gone to town. As we move back into the party room, the staff are entering in a procession, one after the other, carrying trays with lighted sparklers around the edges piled high with food. Everyone crowds around as they place them on a long table covered with a white tablecloth. It looks amazing.

There are the prawn and asparagus flans I'd loved so much in Spain; toasts decorated with chorizo, olives, goats' cheese and peppers; tortilla chips with a variety of dips; anchovies, squid and tiny fish in breadcrumbs; lots of different cheeses; bowls full of sun-dried tomatoes and crispy patatas; thick slices of tortilla; platters of cold meats and sardines; baskets of different breads; and plates of sweet pastries, sugary doughnuts and the delicious little cakes I'd grown so fond of.

All of them recommended by Abuela over the phone. She had insisted on dictating every single one of the recipes to us; it had taken her ages. Her granddaughter's mobile phone bill will be off the wall. Worth it though. The chef was delighted when we passed them on to him.

Concha and I grin at each other as all around us people shriek with delight.

'¡Perfecto!' exclaims Señor Hairy Ears, and Miss Martínez beams from ear to ear and gives Concha and me a hug.

'It was my idea too!' lies Pablo and she flips her hand at him instead. Everyone laughs.

'Can we start?' asks someone and Miss Martínez, carried away by the pleasure of the moment, says, 'I don't see why not,' and then realizes her mistake as everyone grabs a plate and starts piling food on to it as fast as they can.

'Line up!' she shrieks, and an orderly queue forms. Soon everyone is sitting down and tucking in, including the mums and dads who have wandered back in from the bar clutching glasses and bottles of wine. At the table next to us, Jude perches on Pablo's knee and feeds him bits of tapas.

'Look at those two!' growls Concha, her arms folded in outrage. She's so angry she hasn't touched the plate of food in front of her. 'It makes me want to vomit!'

'Look at them instead then!' I nod in the direction of Holly's mum and dad who have sat down at a table across the room. They are deep in conversation, catching up on lost time, I guess. As we watch, he tops up her wine and she smiles at him. Then they pause and clink their glasses together like they're celebrating something important, just the two of them, in their own little world.

They must be back together again. Thank goodness! A wave of relief washes over me. None of this sordid little affair with my mother ever needs to come to light now. Concha is the only person I've told and tomorrow she goes home. Anyway she wouldn't tell anyone, she'd promised.

But though I'm weak with relief, deep down I'm cross too. Where does this leave my poor mum? Does she know it's over between them? And what would have happened if she'd been here? Would he have been with her instead? Or would the two mums have been fighting over him, the hottest guy on Planet Anorak?

Suddenly my arm is gripped so tightly I jump. 'Ow! What are you doing?'

Beside me, Holly is rigid with excitement. 'I knew it! I knew if I could get them talking again they'd sort out their differences!' she squeals. 'They've made up, I can tell!'

Her face shines with happiness. Parents! I wonder if her dad has a clue what he's been putting her through?

'Come here you!' I say and pull her towards me, squeezing her tight in a huge, congratulatory hug. Little does she know I'm as relieved about this as she is. Behind her back, Concha winks at me complicitly. Then her face changes and she says, 'Uh-oh!'

'What's wrong?' asks Holly, sitting upright.

'Your mum's just arrived, Jaime,' says Concha.

'What?' I turn towards the door and see Mum standing alone, peering short-sightedly into the darkness of the room, and I freeze. She's supposed to be safely out of the way tonight, having dinner with Concha's dad! I groan aloud. 'What's *she* doing here?'

'Don't be horrible!' says Holly. 'Over here, Mrs Packer!' She jumps up to wave wildly at my mother. Around the room everyone, including her dad, looks up to see who Holly is shouting at. I groan inwardly as Mum catches sight of us and makes her way towards our table. Holly pulls her down to sit next to us.

'I thought I'd call in on the way home,' explains Mum. 'See how you're all getting on. How were the tapas?'

'Great!' says Concha, pushing her plate towards her. 'Try some!'

'Not for me,' says Mum, patting her tummy. 'I've been out for dinner, remember?'

'You look fantastic,' says Holly.

'Thank you,' smiles Mum. 'You seem happy tonight.'

'I am,' she says conspiratorially. 'My mum and dad are back together again.'

Beside me, I can feel my mother stiffen. 'That's wonderful,' she says faintly. 'When did all this happen?'

'Tonight. Look, they're over there.' Holly points at her mum and dad who are staring at us from the opposite side of the room. Her mum smiles and waves. Her dad raises his hand. Mum, zombie-like, raises hers in return. 'Well, I don't know for definite,' Holly prattles on, 'but I'm pretty sure they are. They've been together all night, haven't they, Jaime?'

'Yep.' I look at Mum who's still as a waxwork next to me, her face taut and pallid, and say flatly. 'Great news, isn't it?'

'Wonderful,' repeats Mum. 'Marvellous.' Her voice is different now, quiet and strained, and both Concha and Holly glance at her curiously.

Suddenly I have a sinking, horrible feeling in the pit of my stomach that it's too late. It's going to come out, all of it. Mum's going to fall apart and Holly's going to put two and two together and work out what's been going on. I sit there, fraught with tension, waiting for the storm to break. Mum clears her throat and my eyes dart to hers, pleading with her not to cause a scene.

She looks at me for a few seconds, puzzled, then her eyes widen with understanding. She knows that I know what's been going on.

The next second she's jumped to her feet. 'I'm going to the loo,' she announces. 'Won't be a tick.' We all watch as she walks across the room, neat and stylish in her black dress, but only I can tell how upset she is by how stiffly she holds herself.

As she disappears into the Ladies, Holly remarks thoughtfully, 'She looks gorgeous tonight, your mum. Dressed to kill. Are you sure she hasn't got a fella?'

'No,' I say fervently. 'She's not going out with anyone.' But I'm scared it's not enough because I can sense Holly's eyes boring into me like she can see inside my head and my cheeks let me down as usual, I can feel them starting to burn.

And then Concha butts in.

I should never have trusted her. I might have known she'd let me down. She was just biding her time to get back at me for going with Pablo.

'Tell Holly the truth, Jaime,' she says, her voice all serious, like she really cares. 'Tell Holly who your mum's been going out with.'

I gaze at Concha wild-eyed, willing her to stop, but it's no good. She's got herself an audience now. Not just Holly, by the way, oh no! Fern, Dolores, Ana, Adam, Jason, Sergio, you name them, every single person who matters to me is sitting round that table, waiting to hear who my mother has been dating. And none of them will ever speak to me again when they find out.

Even Pablo and Jude have tuned in at the next table and they don't even know my mum! And I swear Miss Martínez, who is sitting next to them, is earwigging too.

'Concha!' I plead. 'You said you wouldn't tell . . .'

'You told Concha and not me?' says Fern, hurt.

'I'm sorry!' I whisper and my heart sinks as she looks even more offended and Dolores puts her arm around her.

Holly pouts. 'She never told me neither,' she says sourly to Fern, as if I'm not there. 'She knew what I was going through with my dad and she never said a thing.'

'I know,' I say miserably.

'So why would you do that?' continues Holly, addressing me directly now, belligerent with suspicion. 'Why didn't you tell me your mum was seeing someone? I told you about my dad.'

'It hasn't been going on for long,' I say, praying she would stop jabbing at me with her questions, knowing that she wouldn't until the truth turned round and smacked her in the face.

'Just tell us who it is!' groans Adam. 'Put us out of our misery.'

I shake my head in distress.

'I'll tell them,' says Concha.

'No!'

'Shut up, Concha, it's none of your business,' says Pablo quietly and Concha darts him a look of pure venom. Thanks, Pablo, I am sooo grateful for your support but it's too late. Vengeful, attention-seeking, limelight-craving Concha is savouring this moment to the full.

'Oh yes it is,' she says, her tone like saccharine. 'Anyway, I'm surprised you haven't worked it out by now.'

'Please, Concha!' I say desperately but she ignores me.

'You want to know who it is?' she says goadingly to the rest of the table. 'Well then, take a look over there. It's him if you must know.'

She nods meaningfully across the room, and as the whole table turns to look I close my eyes and wait for the gasps of outrage as everyone discovers that my mum is Holly's dad's bit on the side.

But to my surprise, there are none, just a few intakes of breath and chuckles and 'Aahhs!' of understanding.

Do they approve of this? Do they think it's funny?

I open my eyes and see a man standing at the door.

It's Señor Gómez.

As we watch, my mum comes out of the loo and greets him, pointing in our direction. Señor Gómez offers her his arm and escorts her across the room to our table.

'Had a nice date?' asks Concha sweetly. Mum laughs nervously and Señor Gómez beams and says lots of 'Yeses' and 'Thank yous' and 'Very goods', his head like a nodding dog's.

'Good dinner?' I ask and Mum sits down and launches into a detailed description of the menu which is so boring everyone soon loses interest and goes back to their own agendas. Señor Gómez manages to find a seat next to Miss Martínez and devotes his attention to her.

Beneath the table I grab Concha's hand and squeeze it tight.

'Gracias,' I mouth. 'Gracias, amigo.'

The exchangees leave by coach the next morning. It's an emotional send-off, with all the girls sobbing on each other's shoulders and promising to stay in touch for ever and all the boys larking about, wrestling and tripping each other up, which I think is their way of saying they're sad too. Pablo, being older and more in touch with his feelings, comes up and gives me a big hug.

'Goodbye, my beautiful teacher, my beautiful friend,' he says, which makes me blush, Concha scowl, and Fern and Holly say, 'Aahh!' But then he spoils it by grabbing Jude who's turned up to say goodbye and snogging her right there in front of us all. Everyone cheers because it goes on for ever and in the end Señor Hairy Ears has to intervene to break them up. I laugh with everyone else, but inside I feel awful and I know Concha does too even though she manages to wave to Ana and Dolores when they shout, 'See you in Spain, Concha!' as they board the coach.

'Your turn next,' I say, turning to her as the coach disappears round the corner. 'Come on, we'd better get off home. Your dad's booked us a taxi to the airport in an hour's time.'

She wrinkles her nose. I don't think she wants to go. Fern comes up between us and tucks her arm through ours, looking forlorn. She's missing Dolores already.

'Why didn't you two tell me your mum and dad were going out together?' she grumbles as we walk down the road together.

I shrug, wishing she'd change the subject until Señor Gómez is safely back in Spain. 'Embarrassed, I suppose. You know me.'

'Why? I mean, personally I think it's dead romantic. Don't you, Holls?' Holly has caught up with us and is hanging off my other arm, tuning in to the conversation.

'What's romantic?'

'Jaime's mum and Concha's dad getting it together. Don't you think it's sweet?'

Sweet? She hasn't a clue. Her mum being securely conjoined to her dad, she has no idea how scary it is to be in charge of a single mother.

'Nah, I'm with Jaime on this one,' says Holly morosely.

'It's mega-embarrassing when your aged parent goes on the dating scene.'

'I'm so glad your mum and dad are back together again,' I say fervently.

Her face breaks into a grin. 'Me too,' she says. 'I feel better already. I'm going to try harder at school now, stop messing about. Can I borrow your maths book to copy up the homework?'

We all burst out laughing and she says, 'What?' For Holly this is progress.

'Did you ever find out who it was he was seeing, Holly?' continues Fern with her one-track mind.

I can't help it, I feel cold, freezing cold. I have to repress the urge to shiver.

'Nope. Some old slapper, I suppose. He won't talk about it. It's like it never happened.'

The blood rushes to my face and I feel hot, boiling hot. Now I have to repress the urge to slap Holly right across the face!

Some old slapper.

That's my mum you're talking about!

But Holly doesn't know that, does she? And she never will. With difficulty I get my anger back under control.

In the taxi on the way to the airport Concha is quiet, but as soon as we get there, she starts acting up. She goes on and on about how she's starving even though Mum had done her a massive cooked breakfast before we left. She demands money to spend in the shops, then she whines because the plane is delayed half an hour and she's fed up of waiting. She's like a big spoiled kid, everything is wrong, just like she was at the beginning when I arrived in Spain. She's getting on everyone's nerves. Mum is surprised because she hasn't seen that side of her before and her father looks as if he'd like to throttle her.

'I am sorry,' says Señor Gómez as she wanders out of earshot. 'The truth is, Concha is very sad to be leaving. She cannot cope with emotion, especially goodbyes. Since her mother left . . .' His voice trails away as Concha reappears, scowling.

'You might as well go,' she says grumpily to Mum and

me. 'No point in us all hanging round here wasting time.'

'I suppose not,' says Mum. 'Hug?' and she stretches her arms out towards her. Concha stands there ignoring her, a haughty expression on her face, so Mum laughs, steps forward and enfolds her in her arms. 'I'm going to miss you, Grumpy Guts,' she says, patting her back and pressing her face into Concha's mop of black hair, and suddenly, Concha lets out a strangled howl and flings her arms around Mum's neck.

By the time she's managed to prise herself away from Mum and say goodbye to me, all trace of grumbling, glowering Concha has vanished. She's a sobbing, squelching, blubbery mess and I'm a bit mushy myself.

'Thank you,' I whisper, hugging her to me.

'What for?'

'Keeping my secret.'

She hugs me back tightly like she'll never let me go. 'I don't want to go,' she whispers back. 'I want to stay here.'

'No you don't.' I try to jolly her along. 'You've got Pablo at home. He's all yours now.'

'I don't want him!' she protests fiercely. 'You can have him!'

'I don't want him either!'

We both laugh But it's true, in my case, though, I'm not so sure about Concha. I don't want him any more. I'm off men and their cheating ways.

'I'm going to miss you,' she says.

'You'll be all right. You've got mates in Spain.'

'No I haven't.'

'Yes you have. You've got Dolores and Ana. They're friends with you now.'

'You reckon?' She looks a tad happier. Beside us, her father glances at his watch, does his bow and clicky heels thing and kisses Mum and me on both cheeks.

'Time to go, Concha,' he says and Mum and I watch as they walk together through the door to Departures. At the last minute, Concha turns and gives us a forlorn little wave and then they're gone. Mum's eyes well up.

'Poor little kid,' she says softly to herself. 'We parents have got a lot to answer for.'

'Mum?' She's so lost in thought I touch her arm and she looks at me with sad, surprised eyes as if she's forgotten I'm there.

'Yes?'

I lick my lips. I don't want to ask this question but I have to.

'It's finished, isn't it? You and . . . Holly's dad?'

At last it's out in the open. The words lie exposed between us like a raw, inflamed wound and there's no taking them back. If she denies it, it will fester away for ever. It's up to her now.

Mum closes her eyes. 'Yes,' she says flatly. 'It's over.'

'It's OK.' I don't want her to be sad. 'Don't say any more. That's all I wanted to know.'

'You were never meant to find out.' She smiles at me ruefully. 'I'm sorry, Jaime.'

'I'm sorry too for behaving like a brat.'

She sighs deeply. 'I didn't realize till I saw your face last night exactly what I'd put you through.'

'What did you see in him?' I say curiously, then add quickly, 'Sorry, I shouldn't ask.'

She shrugs, at a loss. 'I don't know. Someone to talk to? A chance to dress up and go out at last? Someone who was interested in me for once?'

Suddenly I understand how lonely my mum has been all these years. What right did I have to keep her to myself?

'There's plenty more fish in the sea,' I say comfortingly, taking her hand and lacing my fingers through hers like I used to do when I was little. 'You can do better than him!'

She laughs and squeezes my fingers back. 'You reckon?' she says and she sounds exactly like Concha, sort of doubtful but hopeful at the same time. 'Listen to you, doling out all the advice. I should be saying these things to you.' Her voice softens. 'I think I know how keen you were on Pablo.'

'*Were*,' I echo regretfully.

'Do you want to talk about it?'

I hesitate, then suddenly I open up. 'The trouble is, Mum, Pablo's a bit like Holly's dad. He's got too much of a roving eye. Not my type. Me, I'm into monogamy. From now on I'm on the lookout for a strictly One-Woman kind of man.'

'Me too. They say the best way to get over a man is to move on to the next one. But personally I can think of a much better way to mend our broken hearts.'

Suddenly there's a glint in her eye and I wonder what this mother of mine is going to come out with next.

'Something we missed out on earlier this year?' she hints. 'Good Friday tradition?'

She's got me foxed now. 'What's that?' I ask, puzzled.

'A bit of retail therapy?'

'YEAH!' How could I forget? 'Bring it on!'

'OLÉ!' she shouts and, OK, we're attracting far more than our fair share of attention but I couldn't care less. Those days of blush alert are well and truly consigned to my childhood. I tuck my arm into my mum's and we stride purposefully through the exit doors, heading for a taxi to take us to the shops, giggling our heads off.

Two women.

Together.

Summer holidays. Bliss. Usually I'm bored to tears, stuck at home with Mrs Bick for company, but things have changed now. This year Mum has finally left me to my own devices and it's been fantastic.

'I suppose if you're old enough to go to Spain on your own, you're old enough to look after yourself at home,' she'd said doubtfully as she stocked the fridge full of food so I wouldn't starve to death while she was at work. She spent the first few days phoning me every five minutes to check up on me, which was a bit of a pain when you're out with your mates, as I kindly pointed out to her. Then she'd got a bit shirty and said that ACTUALLY, if I had nothing better to do than hang around with my friends all day long, maybe I should take over the shopping and cooking while she was at work and, come to think of it, I could hang the washing out and put the hoover over once in a while as well. Blooming cheek!

I suggested, quite sensibly I thought, that she paid me for it because she wouldn't let me get a job even though I'm fourteen and EVERYONE else has got one (well, not Fern, her mum won't let her have one either, but Holly helps in the hairdresser's two days a week, it's not fair), and this led to a fairly heated discussion when Mum pointed out that she'd been doing all these things for me all my life so maybe *I* owed *her* a bit of back pay.

Then we both calmed down and I said I was sorry and she gave me a hug and told me she had a surprise for me. And it turned out she'd booked a holiday in Spain for us both.

'Are we going to stay with Concha and Señor Gómez?' I asked, thrilled to bits, and she said, 'Good grief no! We're going to a hotel on the Costa Brava for sun, sea and sand!' and I was even more excited then, though for a moment I nearly died because I thought she was going to say, 'Sun, sea and sex!' and I couldn't cope with that, not from my own mother, even if it was a joke!

We had a fabulous time, the hotel was brilliant, there was loads to do and stacks of people to go around with even though the only ones I could practise my Spanish on were the waiters because everyone else was either British or German. It didn't feel a bit like the real Spain but I had a good laugh hanging out with my new holiday mates.

Mum enjoyed it too; I've never seen her so happy and relaxed, she chatted to everyone. It was the first time I'd seen her in a bikini for years and I have to admit, she looked pretty good considering she's pushing forty. When I told her that she laughed and said, 'Forty's the new thirty!' and ordered another piña colada. Then the next night she went out for dinner with this single guy called Clive who was staying at our hotel.

He was quite tasty in a middle-aged way, better than Holly's dad anyway, though we don't mention that any more. The next day we were all by the pool, Mum and Clive topping up their tans and me chilling out with some mates, when Clive asked me to take a photo of him and Mum. They posed grinning for the camera like a proper couple, him sitting behind her on the lounger, and I couldn't help but notice he had one hand round her bare waist and the other resting on her hip. It freaked me out a bit to be honest, but it was OK, he was flying home that night.

Then later on I was mucking about with this guy called Jake and Mum came up to talk to us. I didn't even fancy him, he was just a friend, but he had his arm round me, like you do, and I was in my bikini, natch, and I noticed Mum checking *me* out this time, just like I did with her. How weird is that?

It's made me think, you know, now we're home again,

just how much things have changed between Mum and me this year. Like, the gap has narrowed somehow.

She's not my ancient, boring Mum any more. And I'm not her shy little girl who goes red if anyone looks at her, and that's cool.

But for both of us it'll take a bit of getting used to.

Telling You Straight

Sign up to the competitions

Be the first to know about the new books

Get sneak peeks

Talk to Chris Higgins

www.chrishigginsthatsme.com
www.hodderchildrens.co.uk